I0626163

Dead Reckoning
And Other Stories

David M. Kelly

www.davidmkelly.net

Dead Reckoning And Other Stories

Copyright © 2015 by David M. Kelly

ISBN-13: 978-0-9938890-5-9
ISBN-10: 0-9938890-5-0

www.davidmkelly.net
Email: writing@davidmkelly.net

First Published 2015 by
Nemesis Press
Wahnapitae, Ontario

www.nemesispress.com

Printed in U.S.A

Dedication

*To my first reader, my best friend and
biggest supporter – my wife, Hilary.*

Contents

Dead Reckoning

Hector Tren-Hump smiled as he lay on the dais waiting to die. The projected MemChron of his life flashed around him as his memories were downloaded, cataloged and indexed one-by-one into the glowing LifeCube hovering just above his forehead. Now and then he heard the gasps and collective ooh's of his assembled family as the Cataloging threw up a LifeScene they recognized.

He laughed as an image of Miley-Ellyn filled every screen, her chubby face looming close as he held his first born, moments after she'd entered the world. The delicious scent of her fresh baby skin replaced a few seconds later by the stench of cheap cigars. Monty, his first business partner appeared, skinny features whitened and drawn.

"You can't Hector, it's not right. You can't fire people just because they strike…"

"Of course *we* can," Hector sneered. "Effective human capital management will optimize our profits to over three hundred million. How can that be wrong?"

Monty's eyes were wide. "But it'll cost over fifty thousand jobs."

"Sure, sure. And ten thousand Thingamese that would otherwise starve get work. Sentiment has no part in business.

You know that, Monty."

"But the Unions? They won't stand by and let this happen."

Hector let out a disparaging grunt. "Those guys are like anyone else. All you need is the right leverage."

"You can't buy *everyone*, Hector."

"Says who?"

"And the virtual services? We said they were free and now we're selling the clients down the drain to every marketing company going." Monty scowled.

"Those idiots? Listen, if you're not the one paying, you're the one getting sold. Even a half-wit knows that."

Another montage of LifeScenes appeared as the memory of Monty blurred with many similar ones, the Cataloger automatically indexing the events according to the priority Hector's neural pathways gave them.

Hector lingered on the deal with Monty. Damn he was proud of that. They'd made a commission of fifteen million each that year alone. Monty had handed his share over to some ridiculous charity, but for Hector it was a stepping stone to more extensive projects with ever bigger percentages. That was what had put him in the position he was in now.

As the brochures said, MemChron was just the beginning.

After all, anyone with the smarts to put together a couple of hundred K could afford MemChron. Then, when the big day came, they could parade their LifeScenes in front of family and friends, recording them so that their nearest and dearest had a complete record of their life experiences.

So what? Like life insurance, it didn't help *you*.

But, if you wanted something *really* special…

"As one of our Select Mortizens you will enjoy unparalleled freedom to indulge yourself in Elyzium. LifePlus has over thirty years' experience in assisting our clients to live their deaths to the fullest. We honor the people we serve with quality as our cornerstone and integrity, respect and compassion as our building blocks. It's like Life, only more so."

What did they say? If you have to ask the price, you can't

afford it. But, if you *could*, there was Ascendance.

"Yes Sir, Mr. Tren-Hump. Ascendance in no way interferes with your life-span; you are absolutely guaranteed to get every second coming to you. In fact you may get a few seconds not coming to you." Indulgent chuckle. "Once diagnosed as terminal and, with your consent of course, you'll be brought in to LifePlus Inc's own facilities, where you'll be given the utmost care."

"First, you're stabilized so that we can manage the LifeScene Cataloging. It's a beautiful ceremony, Sir. I can tell you that many times I've wept at a client's cataloging. Family and friends can attend, of course. Some clients like to invite their hmmm... rivals too, in order to... share... the glory of Ascendance."

"Once brain core shutdown is detected, the final transfers are completed and your new life begins. You become a LifePlus Select Mortizen, maintained forever in our Elyzium servers. You can continue life's journey for as long as you care to, free to pursue your interests, free to indulge your ambitions and desires in *any* way you choose."

"Yes, of course, Sir, you can keep in contact with your family. Most Select members find they enjoy themselves so much they don't feel it necessary, but that's entirely at your discretion."

Hector rubbed his wizened hands along the fine grained leather of his luxurious chair; he would even be able to keep his feckless son in check.

"That's right, Sir. Now if you would just care to make your gene imprint here..."

Gloating over his enemies wasn't necessary; out-existing them was revenge enough for Hector. All he wanted was to ensure he — and his fortune — *continued*. As a Mortizen, he had no real power, but he had no doubt he could direct his descendants appropriately.

The rousing strains of the classic "My heart will go on" lilted from hidden speakers and tears welled up in Hector eyes.

The LifeScene showed him marrying Kaydianne, despite both his children's objections and his first wife's tears. Kaydianne's cleavage swelled up on the display, filling his world with a pink flesh sky, her heady perfume warming his nostrils, and then...

Snap!

A white-hot pain burned through Hector's chest and head; for one brief second he was overwhelmed by agony roiling up his spine and cauterizing every nerve.

No, wait. Maybe this isn't such a good idea after all. Can I think this over a little longer? His mind skittered in fear.

Snap!

A second stab of agony completed the transfer. The pain was gone. The ache in his limbs that had been there for at least twenty years was gone. The stabilization-induced torpor was gone too.

And so were his clothes.

While the first three items were blessings and made him want to jump around screaming like a madman, the idea of wandering naked around the virtual heaven of LifePlus Inc's Select community bothered him. He'd have settled for just about anything, even a pair of pajamas. He had a beautiful pair of dark red silk ones Kaydianne had bought him. She said they made him look just like Bublé in all those classic movies, a little heavier perhaps but...

Hector's confusion grew as he examined himself. He had the same body he'd died in. Where was the twenty-four year old hunk-body he'd never had, but ordered? And why *didn't* he have any clothes? Dark red silk, gray woolen worsted, a pair of jeans and a T-shirt promoting General ToyoSan Motors would have been acceptable. Where was his luxury villa, complete with swimming pool and maid service?

Instead he gazed down on a flabby chest, gray-hair covered man-breasts, flaccid arms and thighs. This wasn't what he'd signed up for. Glowing letters flared up inside his vision, but they were meaningless:

Tren-Hump, Hector. TH15D3AD-1485-13A6-5661A946B3101857
Cycles: 1   CPU Credit: 1%   Ducks: 0.0

Snap!

Hector jumped, his body arching reflexively. This wasn't the same moment of disconnection he'd experienced during the transfer; this was a blistering pain that cut across his back as though his spine had been ripped out.

"Okay, Noob. Time to get all those gleaming new Hoxels dirty."

The creature facing Hector was huge: a powerful humanoid at least three meters tall with four arms and a physique that would have made the Hulk turn white.

"I'm Marshal, but you call me Sir, and make sure you shout it loud so there's no mistake."

"What the hell's going on here — yeow!" Hector squealed again as the whip snapped out and flayed across his shoulders. Virtual or not, the pain felt like his skin had been torn from his body.

"SIR!"

Hector cowered, the searing pain in his back throbbing mercilessly. "What the hell's going on here, Sir?"

Again the whip lashed out and Hector screamed.

"And be respectful when you speak to me," bellowed the Marshal. The whip flicked several times like a cat swishing its tail but didn't land a blow. "Join the line and get ready to do some heavy duty Judgment."

"Judgment? Ahhhh!" The whip lashed out again, wrapping around Hector's flabby torso and slicing pain across his midriff. "You've no idea who I am, do you? I'll make your life a living hell by the time I'm done."

Crack! The whip coiled around Hector's neck and he was jerked to the floor at the feet of the giant. A booted foot pressed down on his throat, threatening to choke the life out of him. A blistering agony erupted in his right buttock and he squirmed in a pathetic attempt to escape as the Marshall pressed what seemed to be a branding iron against him.

Just as Hector felt he couldn't take any more the pressure on his neck lifted. "You Noobs are so funny. Your ass officially belongs to me. Now get in line before my sense of humor runs out. I didn't pay all those Ducks to waste it on the likes of you."

Hector spotted a group of other naked people close by, each one with an angry red mark somewhere on their buttocks. He joined them, nodding in reflex at a couple of people who looked vaguely familiar.

A mistake had been made and when he got to the bottom of it, heads were going to roll. By God, he'd make sure of that.

The Marshal glowered at them. "You disgust me. Why did you come here if you can't even afford the basics like clothes? I can't bear to look and you're going to get everyone else so upset they can't Judge properly. Here."

An itchy sensation developed in Hector's groin as a set of black crotch-hugging shorts appeared; the tightness gave him the distinct feeling that he looked even more naked wearing them. Worse, they chafed like the roughest haircloth when he moved.

The Marshal marched forward, singing loudly and badly off-key.

"You thought you were going to play." The group shuffled along behind him, echoing his tortured chant.

"In your paradise every day."

"You have got a lot to learn."

The man next to Hector whispered, "Sing along or we'll all get it."

"We have got so much to learn," they chorused.

"If you don't, I'll make you squirm."

"If we don't he'll make us squirm."

"Sound off."

"One. Two."

"Sound off."

"Three. Four."

After what seemed like hours, the Marshal led them into a large building segregated into an infinite number of identical cubicles. They reminded Hector of the stark interiors of several companies he'd owned. Occasionally he'd been forced to put in an appearance at one or another; sometimes to reassure a whining workforce but more often to implement classic management strategy by planting fear, uncertainty and doubt.

"Take the first empty cube on your right. Someone will give you your assignments," the Marshal boomed, his voice magnified far beyond the point of human capacity.

"What if we don't?" Hector regretted the words as soon as he spoke; and regretted them even more when the whip cracked over his raw back again. Before anything else could happen he took the first empty cube on his right.

His cube was a featureless gray box designed to fulfill the most basic functionality and not one iota more. Nevertheless, Hector slid into the chair with a sigh as if it were the most luxuriously upholstered Lay-Z-Boy, still wincing at the pain in his buttocks. The march had drained his strength, though he couldn't understand how he could feel tired here. He was now a virtual MemChron pattern living inside a Zettabyte virtual environment, maintained by thousands of banks of volumetric image processors.

A head poked around the door, the fat dark features rife with boredom. "I am Fetch. Your projects are: A4718DV, T9901TM, B64589SA, W7652LK, C5677KL, F1529TY…" The figure reeled off at least another fifty other codes. "The sooner you are being started, the sooner you will be getting finished."

"Start what?"

The rotund head vanished but reappeared seconds later. "You are having been recruited for Judgment. That is your direction."

The Marshal had mentioned Judgment, but Hector had no idea what it was. "I don't know what's going on here, but there's been a mistake. I'm Hector Tren-Hump, a Select

LifePlus member and I *demand* to be put in contact with a representative from LifePlus Inc. immediately."

Fetch smiled. "Ah… you want to be speaking to LifePlus? Why did you not be saying so?"

This sounded more promising, Hector thought. Now he'd sort out this mess. His LifePlus lifestyle was out there waiting for him and he was eager to get on with it.

"Welcome to the LifePlus Incorporated Select Member helpline. Your new life starts here."

Hector jumped as the display appeared from nowhere, floating in his vision like an afterimage caused by staring at something too long. The all-too perfect features of a virtual host filled his vision with milky white skin. "It's about time. Someone has made a big mistake and I don't believe in forgiveness. I'm Hector Tren-Hump and I de-"

"Our office hours are 10:00:00 to 10:00:01 UT. Please leave a message after the tone."

The long beep reminded Hector of the moment in TriVid crime shows when a key character died after a long and pointless coma. He was completely unprepared for the messaging system and missed the opportunity. "One second? Their operating hours are one second? What the hell am I supposed to do with that?" Hector asked, not expecting an answer.

"You should be leaving a message of course," Fetch chuckled. "Now please be working on your projects. We are making allowances for you being a Noob. But we could just be doing *this*."

A jolt of pain shot through his still raw buttocks and danced agonizingly upwards. Hector squawked and tried to clamber off the chair but was stuck to the seat.

"Judgment," Fetch commanded. "You are having your assignments."

"Wait. How do I call back?" Hector felt his strength drain, a feeling that worsened with each beat of his pulse. "I need to leave a message."

"We are having a one call per cycle limit to the Help-desk."

Hector collapsed over the featureless desk top, his head falling into the nest of his arms.

"Hey, you…"

Hissed words drifted over the top of the cubicle from the adjoining one.

"If you don't work, you ain't going to make it."

"Me? Who? What?" Hector struggled to think coherently; a chill seemed to envelop him from nowhere. "Who're you?"

"I'm your Fairy Godmother, of course. You ain't given enough SeePeeYoo for a whole cycle. You have to work. Otherwise you'll get Hibernated and you really wouldn't enjoy that."

"Hibernated?" Hector struggled to respond.

"Okay bud. You need a shot or you're not even going to get through this conversation. You need to do some work." The voice hesitated. "Why the hell I should care, I don't know. See the gray patch on the right? Swipe your hand over it. That'll activate your console. You'll get enough of a boost that we can carry on talking."

Hector scanned the desk top but struggled to focus. "It's all gray…"

"Sure, sure. If it was easy it wouldn't be work, now would it?"

Hector scraped his hand over the desk in vague gestures, the slight texture almostt imperceptible against his skin; it seemed useless but he tried. Just as he felt he was going to pass out, a glowing square appeared. At the same time he felt a new-found strength course through his body. "Wow. That feels better." Hector stretched in his seat. "Maybe I can get out of here now."

"Listen, you dope. All you've done is activate your screen; that's given you enough SeePeeYoo to keep you going a couple of minutes maybe. Check your DUD."

"DUD?"

"Dead-Up-Display. Geez. It tells you what your SeePeeYou is. Once that's gone, you're Hibernated."

Hector realized the voice was talking about the display inside his vision. The CPU reading was at half a percent.

"So what's Hibernation?"

"You'll find out if you're not careful. Just think of it as the worst place you don't want to be."

Hector swore to himself. "Okay, okay. I don't want to be Hibernated. I get it. What do I do?"

"You work. Use the controls and screen to play the Judgments. Each one you complete earns you SeePeeYoo. Complete your quota and you earn enough not to get Hibernated and you-"

"And I don't want to be Hibernated. Give it a rest will you?" Hector wasn't paying much attention; he needed to contact the outside. Whatever had gone wrong had better be fixed quickly, or he'd make sure people lost their jobs.

"If you're so smart I'll save my SeePeeYoo and leave y..."

"Wait. I didn't mean that. What controls? I don't see anything."

Gray on gray, naturally. If it was easy, it wouldn't be work, Hector thought.

Silence dragged on and Hector was convinced his unseen ally had deserted him. The weakness crept back, his thoughts and movements slowing much faster than before. "Please?" he hissed.

"Feeling the pinch again huh?" This time the voice had a harder edge to it. "It ain't nice that's for sure."

"So, help me."

Another long silence. Hector's hands slid off the desk on to his lap, replaced by his chin as it collided painfully with the gray surface.

"Call up the projects on the screen. Work through them and you earn SeePeeYoo. The more SeePeeYoo, the happier you'll be."

"I don't remember the codes."

"You think you can forget something you dope?" The voice was scornful. "It's all virtual here. Nothing dies."

Hector swiped at the desk again, the random motions eventually bringing up a list of code numbers like the ones he'd been given earlier. Moving his finger over one area moved the selector down, while another spot moved it up.

It would have taken nothing, he realized, to have the list highlight his assignments. Instead he was forced to remember them. His faceless conspirator had said that he couldn't forget the numbers, which turned out to be true; but recalling each project number took a distinct effort.

Hector managed to find a combination of scratches, slaps and swipes that brought up the project on screen, or at least he thought so. When it ran, it was like watching a soap opera, except every now and then the action would stop and he had to choose what he thought the characters would do next. Will Chester forgive Mary? Will Bart free himself from captivity? Will Bob choose cheesecake or pie? It was the most idiotic way he could imagine spending his time, but the weakness didn't return and it gave him time to think. "I need to make a call. How?" he hissed.

The reply took a while to arrive. "You mean… outside? You need lots of Ducks for that — lots and lots."

"Ducks?"

"Digital Bucks: cabbage, bread, mazuma, gravy, moolah, scratch, clams, wampum-"

"Okay, I get the picture. Do I make Ducks doing this?" Hector hated the voice even though it was helping him.

"Course not, this gets you SeePeeYoo. So you can survive. To earn Ducks you need to do something more valuable."

"Such as?"

"What skills do ya got?" A harsh laugh filtered over the wall. "Lemme guess, you're here because you were a big shot back before you died, like everyone else. So your biggest skill is screwing people over. That ain't a high demand occupation around here. We're the screwees not the screwers."

"There must be something." The paused project demanded action and Hector slapped the controls without thinking about his selection.

"You could go to a HoxelBroker. You might be able to sell some of your body parts. But no doubt you're old like the rest of us. Who wants to buy ugly hoxels?" The voice paused. "Of course, you could try the PimpDaddy..."

Hector had no idea what a PimpDaddy was but the name alone was scary enough for him to shy away from the topic, but he had to find a way to contact the outside. If he could get through to his lawyer, he'd be able to straighten out this mess.

After a time passed that could have been measured in government intervention cycles, the display vanished and nothing Hector did would bring it back.

"Judgment has ended. All operators will vacate now." The booming voice seemed to fill the warren-like building. "Mandatory half-cycle down time begins."

There was no response when Hector called out so he started walking in the same direction as the stampede. For the most part the streets were lined with gray buildings, that looked like the poverty stricken towns he'd been dragged through as a youngster by his salesman father; at one point he was hit by an overpowering smell of cheap carnival hot dogs, but no vendor was in sight. Occasionally the scene was punctuated by a structure of incredible grandeur, with gold-trimmed colonnades soaring to buttress intricately carved roofs. It was like Lexington, Virginia meeting the Las Vegas Strip; Norman Rockwell fused with Dali.

Hector had one immediate goal: the Dead Palace, where the VPs of Elyzium (on a temporary rotating deceased basis) spent a year maintaining residence for legal purposes. He didn't know where it was, but the brochures said it was the biggest building in Elyzium. If he couldn't call out, then he'd have to make them give him what he'd paid for.

Another building caught his attention as he walked. It

was the size of a baseball stadium but made of carved marble, with broad golden steps leading up to massive redwood doors. Flanking the doors was a pair of Red Onyx *somethings,* angels or possibly vampires, towering malevolently over the entrance.

Hector moved closer, trying to read the sign over the door. It looked like "Dead All Over" but the intricate script carving made it difficult. He heard what sounded like a slab being dragged across the floor and then was face-to-face with one of the Angel-Vampires; actually it was more like "eye-to-face" given their comparative sizes.

"Members only," growled the Angel-Vampire, jutting out its pointed chin. "If you're not on the list you can't come in."

"Is that a joke?" Hector couldn't believe it; the last time he'd been denied entry somewhere must have been over sixty years ago.

"Do I..." The Angel-Vampire yawned, baring thirty-centimeter fangs. "...look as if I'm joking?"

Hector stepped back. "I just wondered if any of my friends might be in there."

"Your *friends?*" The Angel-Vampire snorted. "Did you 'ear that Burt? That's a good 'un eh?"

The second Angel-Vampire chuckled; a grating rumble vibrating through the air. "That's a rib tickler and no mistake, Fred. Friends. That's rich. Or rather, it's not."

Both guffawed even louder.

"Wait a second. Are you one of the talent? Talent in the back entrance, see."

"Talent?"

"The talent always goes in the back entrance, eh Fred?"

The Angel-Vampires rocked, their combined laughter hitting about four on the Richter scale.

"Gawd... if I still had tear ducts Burt..."

Hector scuttled away while they were distracted, echoes of hooting and bellowing following him for a long time. Some people sure made a lot out of nothing, he thought.

When he found the "Palace," it was rather smaller than

he'd imagined. Positively modest in comparison to some of the other buildings that he'd passed but, as he knew all too well, power didn't necessarily need to flaunt itself.

Making his way down the long entrance hall, Hector's toes sank into the luxurious carpeting, reminding him that he was almost naked and again his anger burned at being placed in such a position. Dead or not, he deserved respect. By the time he reached the reception desk he was ready to draw blood. "I'm Hec-"

"Mr. Tren-Hump," the pretty assistant smiled in a studied mixture of friendliness and concern. "We've been expecting you."

"You have?" Hector sniffed. "Of course you have. Someone screwed up, didn't they? You'll find I'm not a very forgiving man."

"That's understandable, Mr. Tren-Hump. If you'll just take a number and a seat." The assistant gestured towards a wide gold-framed entranceway.

The spacious vestibule was filled with clusters of elegant padded leather chairs that reminded Hector of his favorite club, and a hint of fragrant butterscotch surrounded him as he sat. He was a little surprised to see no one else waiting; he'd expected a long line-up. He saw a glowing number at the opposite end of the room and checked his snatched ticket; he was next. Perhaps this wouldn't be so bad after all he thought, dropping down into a comfortable seat.

Snap!

Hector woke with a scream and jumped away as the whip seared around his back.

"I told you your ass belongs to me. Get up and get to work. Judgment is here," the Marshal yelled.

"What happened to the Palace?" Hector winced and added, "Sir."

"Line up! Line up!"

A sad looking group gathered and Hector reluctantly

joined them, wary of the Marshal's twitching whip. The DUD appeared, but he still didn't really understand it:

```
Tren-Hump, Hector. TH15D3AD-1485-13A6-5661A946B3101857
Cycles: 2          CPU Credit: 1%          Ducks: 0.0
```

"Noobies think they are the best," the Marshal roared and the line-up echoed him.

"They all think they should be dressed."

"Most arrive completely nude."

The man next to Hector wasn't singing and Hector elbowed him. "Join in."

"They don't know they just got screwed," they chorused.

"Sound off…"

After picking up several more stragglers, Hector was back at the same blank-looking desk in what might have been the same cubicle as before. He waited until the noise settled down.

"You there?" He spoke softly, hoping to just catch the attention of those closest.

"Who's 'you'?"

"Errrr… fairy godmother?"

"Neck off, you pervert."

Hector's strength faded and he flailed at the controls.

"Your project numbers are: G8208LU, S5578SH, O6117LO, O8133CF, E1305GE…"

Bile welled up in his stomach as Hector pulled up the first of the scenarios and started to work through it. It was another exercise in pointless tedium, but his stomach settled immediately. Knowing it was the only thing keeping him going he tried to stay focused, while considering his circumstances.

The day dragged like an election campaign, each project seeming to last hours. Hector could envision an infinite series reaching in to the future. He wondered if he'd just imagined Ascendance. Had he not "made it" and this was… he pushed the idea away not wanting to think about it, but he *was* suffering an apparently never-ending punishment.

When the controls vanished, Hector scrambled to his feet. He was out of the cubicle and hurrying down the street before the voice announcing the end of Judgment had faded. He knew where he was going and was determined to get there before he weakened.

The Palace looked the same as the day before. Hector couldn't stop himself thinking in "days," even though he knew they had no meaning here; the "Cycles" in his DUD seemed to be the closest thing. There wasn't even a Sun, just a general glow that seemed permanently stuck as if it were mid-afternoon.

"Hello again, Mr. Tren-Hump. We've been expecting you back." The assistant smiled at him.

"I'm sure you have. Now I need to get this sorted out, before I-"

"Certainly, Mr. Tren-Hump. If you'll take a number and a seat."

"This is bull," he snapped. "You don't actually help anyone do you?"

"Mr. Tren-Hump?"

"You're just here to give people the run-around."

"If you take a seat, Mr. Tren-Hump, one of our consultants will be right-"

Hector dashed into the waiting room, his heart thumping as he approached the door at the other end. Locked! His fist slammed into the carved wooden surface, but other than an ineffectual thud, it had no effect. "You haven't heard the end of this."

Hector galloped back onto the street. From nowhere a double-weighted line wrapped itself around his ankles, tangling him up and he crashed to the ground.

"Got him!"

Several figures materialized around Hector, all dressed in identical bright red and white clothing. Before he could speak he was punched on the jaw and fell on his back. Then the rest enthusiastically joined in, delivering waves of punches and kicks that made him scream as he curled into a ball for protection.

A final kick hit Hector in the face and consciousness started slipping away as if his SeePeeYoo had run out. Perhaps it had; it never seemed to last very long.

"Hey! This isn't him." The voice sounded distorted.

"Don't talk silly. He was in the target zone and running."

"No. Look here."

Hector sensed movement, but couldn't see what was happening.

"Damn! You're right. Invalid Target ID."

"What now?"

"Catch and release rules apply."

A boot prodded Hector, pressing against a rib he was sure was badly fractured.

"Sorry old chap. Bit of an identification cock-up. No hard feelings, eh?"

Hector's mumbled answer was sharp and brief.

"Yes... ahhhh... well. Never mind. Apologies and all that. Thought the target seemed awfully close to home plate."

"Possible target trace. Seven hundred and fifty meters due East."

A squeaky trumpet sounded. "Come on chaps. Tally ho!"

The figures melted away and Hector was alone again, nauseating waves of pain washing through his body. He tried to release the line around his ankles, but had no strength and his bloody fingers slipped from the knots.

His eyes closed.

Snap!

The whip had an almost comfortable familiarity as it curled around Hector's thigh, raising a stinging red weal. "I'm alive?" In his last few moments of consciousness after the attack, he'd convinced himself it was the end.

Crack!

"Of course you're not alive, noob. Get in line." The Marshal windmilled the whip over his head, ready to deliver another blow.

Hector scrambled to the line-up. To his surprise he didn't ache at all and when he checked no wounds were visible. Not healed — there was no scarring or redness anywhere — just gone, as if erased. This time Hector checked his DUD with greater interest:

```
Tren-Hump, Hector. TH15D3AD-1485-13A6-5661A946B3101857
Cycles: 3          CPU Credit: 1%          Ducks: 0.5
```

For the first time, Hector didn't mind being chivvied by the Marshal and settled down into his cubicle. He'd made some Ducks. By accident, for sure. But he'd done it. Even though his Judgment project list was just as tedious as ever, somehow the rest of his day didn't seem quite as bad. He'd made progress and also had a clue of how he could make more — something *much* more pleasant than being hunted...

When Judgment ended, Hector bolted from his cubicle leaving the shuffling throng far behind. The PimpDaddy turned out to be easy to find. Hector found an arrow floating in mid-air pointing off the street to the Palace saying "PimpDaddy." It was ridiculous that he hadn't spotted it before, but he was starting to realize things changed around him without him being aware of it.

The PimpDaddy's lair was like a Bedouin tent genetically mixed with a '59 Eldorado. Walls were covered in rippling red silk. Doors, surrounds and other structures were edged with chrome and giant metal fins protruded from corners. As he approached, the front door opened like a gaping black mouth. "Hello?" Hector swallowed twice, "Is anyone there?"

A red neon sign flashed 'W lcom ', the darkened "e's" not helping Hector's confidence. Stepping forward, he was engulfed in darkness. As his eyes adjusted he noticed the walls were covered in pictures depicting every imaginable sex act, along with several he didn't even recognize. As he looked closer he realized each one was animated to bring out its full lewdness. He felt an acute itchiness around his groin and hastened further inside.

"Why, come in Sir. Why don't y'all come closer so I can see you?"

Hector moved towards the voice, picking out a large figure draped over a rococo chaise longue surrounded by an entourage kneeling on the floor as if in worship. "Are you the PimpDaddy?"

"Well, I ain't Santa Claus."

The crowd laughed and the PimpDaddy plucked a large apple from a tray held by what looked like a cherub. There was something disturbing in the cherub's smile; something far too suggestive.

"Let me save y'all some time." The PimpDaddy bit deep into the apple and chewed for a few minutes before spitting pips at Hector's feet. "You need Ducks and haven't got the talent to make any. So you figured you'd come and take advantage of the PimpDaddy's well-known generosity."

"I haven't-" Hector was going to say he hadn't heard anything of the sort but stopped himself. "-any ducks, no. Your generosity is more than well-known though… legendary I would say."

The PimpDaddy sneered and took another bite of apple. "My clients have, shall we say aaah, *distinctive* tastes. You wouldn't be able to satisfy their demands."

"You don't know that. What would I have to do?"

The PimpDaddy laughed, joined by his entourage. "How good are you at acting? You know — a little role-play…"

Hector thought about it. He'd been cast as a tree in the "Wizard of Oz" when he was at school, but was replaced with a piece of cardboard after two days. Other than that he'd never done anything remotely along that line. "I'm sure I'll manage," he said.

"Hmmmmm? Y'all probably thinking something like this?"

Hector whimpered as his flesh seemed to ripple and

twist on his bones, as if he was being stretched and reshaped from the inside out. He doubled up at the sensation, gasping and shaking, tears blurring his eyes until it was like looking through molten glass. When the sensation faded it took him several breaths until he could speak. "W...What the hell have you done to me?"

"Done *for* you, you mean." The PimpDaddy snapped his fingers.

Hector blinked several times. For the first time since arriving in Elyzium his crotch wasn't suffering the incessant itching from the shorts. The relief was so great he looked down and — "Wow!" The appendage that greeted Hector wasn't anything resembling his own and the fact that he could see it at all past his stomach was something of a revelation.

He looked up and saw his reflection. A veritable Hector idealized. Every muscle and sinew was pumped and sculptured. Far more Adonis-like than he'd ever approached in life and — he glanced down again — incredibly gifted. "That's more like it." Hector turned back to the PimpDaddy. "I think we can do business. This is how it should have been from the start."

The PimpDaddy held up his hand, as if talking to some unseen listener. "No, Nuns are no problem. Oh, you mean real ones? That could be more difficult in here."

"Yes, my advertising does say I can provide anything, but that's just marketing; it ain't real. What do you mean 'implied contract'? Really? Go ahead, sue me. Y'all have a nice day."

"Some people." The PimpDaddy's teeth flashed in the dim light. "So you like that?"

Hector nodded, still half watching himself in the mirror.

"Well don't get attached to it — it's just a loaner. Hoxels like that cost a lot of Ducks. This is more like what I need."

Hector's body twisted and changed again, not quite as unpleasant as the first time because it was less unexpected, but it still blurred his vision until the transition was complete. When he could refocus, the mirror showed a very different figure. "What the hell?"

"Yes, put him on." The PimpDaddy held up his hand, cutting Hector off. "What's the problem? You don't want to do it anymore? Well, what makes you think you have a choice? Labor withdrawal? Sure go right ahead with that. Hibernation is just so much fun... of course I can. Who's gonna stop me?"

Hector stared at the revealing skin-tight gold lamé dress that struggled to contain the pneumatic, feminine body enhanced in all directions. A cleavage, even bigger than his memories of Kaydianne's, separated large mounds of flesh that jiggled without even the slightest provocation. "You can't do th-" Hector's body changed again.

This time when he recovered he was greeted by the reflection of a Nurse, though her uniform was more revealing than any real one. Another change and he saw a Nun brandishing a whip and handcuffs, then a facsimile of Red Riding hood, then a school teacher, a choirboy and finally a Donkey.

He opened his donkey mouth to protest, but nothing but a soft mewl came out. The PimpDaddy's entourage bellowed louder at every change. Hector's donkey ears turned red with humiliation and he pawed the ground with his hoof.

"So, y'all think you can work with us? I've lots of customers and I'm always looking for new talent."

Hector flattened his ears back, twisting his thick neck to shake his head.

Again the room erupted with laughter. Hector spat contemptuously and shuffled towards the door. He felt something dragging and looked down; equal amounts of disgust and embarrassment flooding through him when he discovered it was his huge phallus plowing through the dirt.

Hoots of derision erupted around him, reaching a level that made any kind of reasoned thought almost impossible. The fur along Hector's back stood upright at the burning shame, but all he could do was waddle away on all fours.

"Y'all come back if you change your mind," the PimpDaddy called. "And don't let the door hit you in the 'Ass' as you leave."

Hector pushed his snout against the door and shuffled

through, suddenly on his own hands and knees in the sandy ground. He felt the now familiar itch of his hairy shorts, an almost welcome sensation under the circumstances.

Snap!

Hector smiled as the whip cracked against his skin. Regardless of the pain, at least it was his own skin — not an animal's hide. "I'm not a Donkey!"

"Don't be so sure. You know the drill," the Marshal growled.

Hector rushed to join the line and started singing along with the Marshal's chant. He studied his DUD:

Tren-Hump, Hector. TH15D3AD-1485-13A6-5661A946B3101857		
Cycles: 4	CPU Credit: 1%	Ducks: 0.5

At least nothing had changed for the worse. His assignments for the day seemed just as dreary as usual and it seemed like hours later when Hector shambled out into Elyzium barely ahead of the rest. Visiting the PimpDaddy had just been more humiliation. He desperately needed more Ducks so he could contact his lawyer, but so far only one thing had worked. He wandered at random until he felt the edge of weakness welling up.

A group of people clustered around a small building off to one side. Hector thought he recognized some of them from the previous day/cycle, then one groaned loudly.

"Oh look, see here. It was an accident old chap. Just one of those things." The hunter moved to intercept Hector. "Are you still put out? Really, it was all licensed. You can't go around blaming chaps over a simple accident that could happen to anyone."

"Where do I sign up?"

The man's eyes darted up and down Hector's semi-naked torso. "Frightfully sorry old man, the club is rather exclusive don't you know. Standards have to be maintained and all that."

"I mean sign up to be hunted."

The man's eyes widened. "You want to be the sport? Well, I'll be…"

"How do I do it?"

"Just tell the chap inside; he'll sort everything out." The hunter grinned and waved his arms. "I say, you chaps. This fellow is a new sport, let him through."

The crowd parted and several people let out cheers and whoops that Hector found rather chilling, even though he tried to take them as signs of encouragement. The formalities were soon done with and "the chap inside" reeled off a long list of rules and observances governing his participation.

Hector drifted off as the list went on. It was simple: the longer he avoided capture, the more Ducks he earned. "Do the people chasing me have any rules?"

"No. But this bunch." The man gestured with his thumb. "They like old fashioned trajectory weapons."

Hector grimaced as the man stabbed a large square box against his shoulder. It felt like hundreds of needles penetrating deep into his arm.

"Okay. You're tagged." The man adjusted the controls in front of him. "And you now have 120 seconds of flight and invisibility."

"Flight? Invisibility?" Hector looked down at his arms and legs. "But…?"

"Let me show ya." The man touched a metallic wand to Hector's temple. "To fly ya do this. To go invisible ya do this."

Hector felt the weirdest sensations inside him; like muscle movements but the "muscles" weren't what anyone would consider part of their anatomy. The results spoke for themselves though as he floated upwards and a moment later, his body disappeared leaving him flailing in the air. He was relieved to find that he could at least still feel his limbs and body movements even if he couldn't see them.

"To switch 'em off, ya do the opposite. Like this."

Hector's body reappeared, his pink flesh fading back into

sight. Then he dropped a few inches, landing on his feet with a grunt. "That all seems okay." Hector tried to sound casual.

"Just remember. You don't wanna run out of flight while ya high up." The man laughed at Hector's expression. "It's messy and doesn't entertain anyone."

"Do I start straight away?"

"Ya got," the man glanced at his controls, "thirty-seven minutes till I release the 'hounds'. This is your waypoint; if ya get there safely you earn maximum Ducks, but don't count on it."

Hector jumped through the door, barreling through the throng. The destination was clear in his mind, as if he had a GPS to guide him. He ran and took the first corner available, the hoots and tally-ho's audible behind him. The next few corners he turned randomly; his first idea was to put as much distance as possible between him and the hunters.

Round the next turn was a market; bustling people would provide the perfect cover. He wondered if he should try and hide among them when a voice sounded inside his head.

"...no quarry shall involve parties of the third part so as to put them in danger of being injured or be hindered in their regular day-to-day activities..."

He was being monitored and of course had to play by the rules. "They don't think I'll last very long. But I'll show them," he muttered.

He sprinted into a passageway several hundred meters long. It was a perfect place to get trapped, but Hector's only alternative was to head back towards his pursuers — which he didn't think was a good tactic. He'd already covered almost a quarter of the distance to his destination. Then again, sometimes pretending to drop back was a tactic he'd often used in business — it could lead your enemy to lower their guard.

Hector wasn't getting tired like before. Despite his activity his SeePeeYou wasn't decreasing, but that was only to make the chase more interesting. He knew it wasn't for his benefit.

Halfway along, Hector started to panic. The distant toot

of a horn told him that the chase was on in earnest. Doorways lined the passage and he threw himself at the nearest, but it was locked. Feet scrabbling for traction in the dust, he tried the next with no better success.

Glancing over his shoulder, Hector saw a figure at the far end and again the horn sounded. A flash of movement, then something sliced through his upper arm. Hector yelped, instinctively clamping the wound with his hand, throwing him off balance. Another blur flashed past where his head had just been and embedded itself in the wall to his left. He wasn't sure, but it looked like a crossbow bolt; his stumble had saved him.

Hector pushed himself upright, his right hand covered in realistic gore, and darted further down the passage. He knew he was presenting a relatively easy target, but without escaping the confines of the passage he had no choice.

He was trying to judge what was happening behind him, but didn't dare look in case he tripped again. He heard a faint hiss and dived, rolling clumsily along the floor until obscured by dust. He triggered his new flight skill and invisibility, hopping on to the building roof on his left.

The move confused his pursuers momentarily and he rattled along the roof, slipping precariously on the terracotta tiles. A loud crack sounded behind him and Hector realized someone had followed him; seconds later a blaze of pain tore through his thigh and he tumbled, bouncing off the roof into a thick blanket of Boxwood.

The prickly hedge stank of old cat pee and raked his skin, but that was nothing compared to the agony in Hector's leg. A metal arrow was buried half way into his thigh, blood seeping from around the shaft. It felt like a sizzling metal rod had been driven through him.

Hector scrabbled to the end of the bushes, trying to be quiet. He knew the hunters were tracking him and he had to give them as little to go on as possible. He poked at the arrow in his leg; in movies the hero always gritted his teeth and pulled them out, though he thought he remembered reading that arrows had to be pushed through because of the barbs. Or were you supposed to leave them in to staunch the flow of blood? In reality, the blood made everything too slick to pull and pushing on it only increased the pain.

Footsteps crunched closer and stopped. "You can come out now. I know you're in there."

Ignoring the order, Hector looked around for some sliver of hope. He guessed he had about fifteen seconds of flight and invisibility left, which didn't seem enough to help unless…

Hector hobbled up to the man, drew back his invisible fist and punched the hunter hard on the nose, laughing when the man fell over. How many years had it been since he'd done anything like that? He must have been a child when he'd last been in a physical fight.

Hector started running, the bolt in his leg making it more of a painful shuffle, but he was moving. Around the next corner he found a large park; it reminded him of the "Garden of the Gods", except there were distinct formal sections partitioned off from the wilder and more rugged areas.

There was more shelter in the park and his destination was also somewhere inside it. Heading straight for the waypoint was undoubtedly the wrong approach, but his options became more limited as he got closer.

A dense thicket on his left offered cover while also minimizing weapons range. Hector limped over as quickly as he could, developing a painful neck ache from constantly looking around. Once obscured by the foliage he relaxed a little. Making it this far was good, but it would be much harder to go all the way.

He followed the bank of a broad stream; which didn't seem to fit with the dry sandy areas he could see through the foliage. Then it came to him. There was no reason for the landscape here to follow "natural" processes. None of it was any more real than he was.

Hector stopped and smiled. The stream ran in the right direction and after all it wasn't as if he could die…

Kneeling on the bank he bent down, hesitating as his nose approached the water. Before his courage failed, Hector thrust his head and shoulders into the cool liquid and inhaled.

His lungs felt like he'd breathed in molten lava and he threw himself backwards as he retched. His ribs seemed to shrink until they were two or three sizes too small and he brayed out a series of water-logged coughs. As an almost pathetic afterthought, he vomited a mixture of nothing mixed with water onto the ground.

"I say old thing. Are you alright?"

Hector recognized the voice before he could see clearly. He was caught. "Fine…" He coughed the words out.

"I'll be dashed! Never seen the sport try to kill itself before it was caught. Are you sure you're not sick?"

Hector nodded, struggling up to his knees. "Yes. Do your worst."

The man lifted a small horn and tooted a victorious trumpet. "Oh well. Tally ho chaps!"

Bludgeons, fists and feet assaulted Hector from all sides. Then the lights went out.

Snap!

Tren-Hump, Hector. TH15D3AD-1485-13A6-5661A946B3101857
Cycles: 5   CPU Credit: 3%   Ducks: 5.5
MAIL

Hector grinned as he saw the figures; five entire Ducks, that was huge! The flashing mail sign caught his attention and he heard a voice.

"Hi, I'm Melody, I'm going to help you with your mail. You have one new message. Think 'Play' to play this message. Think 'Skip' to skip this message. Think 'Delete' to delete this message or think 'Goodbye' to exit the messaging system."

Hector concentrated on thinking "Play."

"Ya progress was 68% which normally would get ya 13.6

Ducks." Hector recognized the ChaseMaster's voice. "But ya broke rule four and as a result forfeit all payment."

Hector swore.

"Did you think 'Skip'?" Melody chimed in.

Hector swore again.

"I'm sorry, I didn't get that; please think 'Yes' or 'No'. Did you think 'Skip'?"

"No!"

"You have one old message. Think 'Play' to play this message. Think 'Skip' to skip this message. Think 'Delete' to delete this message or think 'Goodbye' to exit the messaging system."

Hector recalled the message, desperately trying to contain his anger and think the right words.

"- and so forfeit all payment. Oddly though, the hunt liked ya for some reason and awarded ya five bonus Ducks."

The grunting off-key singing of the Marshal reached Hector and he deleted the message, readying himself mentally for the tedium of Judgment. He'd earned some real money and if he could do it once, by God he could do it again. His fat fist pumped the air until the Marshal glared at him suspiciously. Just wait till Judgment was over.

The blue-white laser pulse burned a dark crater in the wall next to Hector's head. He burst from his position of cover, running as fast as his chubby legs would carry him towards the corner of the building. The air burned as shots erupted on all sides, singeing arcs that persisted on his retina as he ducked and weaved.

The decorative blocks on the building melted as a barrage of shots ripped into the wall fractions of a second behind him. But the damage was no more permanent than his injuries would be and the blocks started to re-form even as Hector glanced at them.

Hector felt a tingling sensation and jumped, the explosion from the rocket catching him in mid-air, tumbling him like a sliver of paper in a windstorm. He careened into a wall and lay stunned while his breath returned and his head stopped spinning. His gut instinct had developed through painful practice and the rocket hadn't hit him directly.

Three heavily-armored figures appeared down the block, weapons at the ready. Hector didn't understand why they needed armor; he was just as helpless as ever. It must comfort them, he decided, or help them act out their fantasies.

It was Hector's thirty-seventh run and he was developing a reputation. Some of the other Mortizens nodded to him or gave him knowing winks as they were rounded up for Judgment. Even the Marshall limited his abuse to ensure Hector was in pristine condition for the matches.

No-one would ever have described Hector as "physical," but a lifetime of double-dealing had provided him with a survival skill that surprised even him. Although he'd never actually reached the goal, he'd provided some of the best hunts anyone could remember.

"You're a sneaky liddle bastard," the ChaseMaster said. "And the punters love it."

It was a double-edged sword. His assignments became increasingly tough, like this one. The hunting party had their choice of any weapons technology and, although Hector had been given increased limits on both flight and invisibility, just a single shot could stop him. At least he was earning enough SeePeeYoo to avoid suffering the tedium of Judgment.

Multiple flashes caught his eye and Hector saw the effervescent trails of two missiles heading in his direction. At the very last instant he triggered both his invisibility and flight, shooting vertically to escape. The explosions erupted under him, a shockwave of heat and dust tossing him around violently.

Hector checked the bearing on his target; it was *that* way and not very far in fact. He had a thought: he'd been catapulted much higher than he'd have gone by choice and was now on a free-fall trajectory. If he could stretch out his fall…

Instinctively he nudged himself in the right direction, providing the smallest of adjustments and slowing his fall to maximize his range. His invisibility wouldn't last either, but without it he was an easy target.

Hector started flipping his visibility on and off at random as he fell, hoping to prevent anyone from targeting him effectively.

The ground rushed up at a dizzying rate and it took all of Hector's nerve to save the last precious seconds of flight. In order to maximize his chances he'd have to wait for the last moment to halt his plunge and that would take everything he had.

An explosion burst ahead of him, gouts of sulfurous flame and smoke buffeting his face; a fraction later a second detonation sprouted behind him. The compression on both sides of his body forced the breath from his lungs and intense pain shot through his ribs. It also squirted him back into the air, like an orange pip squeezed between giant fingers.

That was all the break he needed and Hector used his rapidly diminishing flight to push closer to the target zone. He fell the last few meters, crashing into the ground and tumbling awkwardly. He felt his arm snap but struggled to his feet. Choking on the dust he'd kicked up, he forced himself on toward the target.

He sank to his knees and punched the air in triumph with his good arm.

"You made it." The armored figure sounded peevish. "I'll be damned, you made it."

Hector smiled. It might be a small accomplishment relative to what he'd achieved while he was alive, but it had the sweet taste of victory nevertheless. "Better luck next-"

The armored man shook his head; then shot Hector through the chest.

Snap!

Tren-Hump, Hector. TH15D3AD-1485-13A6-5661A946B3101857
Cycles: 43   CPU Credit: 26%   Ducks: 28.3
MAIL

Hector jerked upright, screaming the scream he would have screamed at the time he was shot; if he'd had any lungs.

He triggered the mail and the voice of the ChaseMaster filled his head.

"G'day mate. Sorry about that. The client accepts that ya won, fair and square. One of 'em got a bit carried away. The thrill of the chase — ya know how it is. Anyway, by way of makin' amends etcetera, he's authorized a bonus payment that you'll get along with this message."

Hector ground his teeth as the display clicked over, adding an extra Duck. "Cheap Bastards." He should have made his way to the chase center for his next assignment but now he had some Ducks he had other things on his mind.

Hector focused on the call connection for his lawyer, using his mental interface to dial the right digits. An image opened up inside his vision much to his relief; he'd wondered if they stopped outside calls — they no doubt could if they wanted.

"Travis-Inge-Badouil associates, how may I help you?"

"Put me through to Inge right away, it's Tren-Hump."

"Tren-Hump? That's not… I'm sorry, Mr. Inge is not in right now."

"Don't mess with me, Fionna. This is Hector Tren-Hump. You know me. I want to speak to my lawyer right away."

"Thank you for calling Travis-Inge-Badouil, have a nice day."

"I'll have y-" Hector balled a fist as the call was disconnected. When he tried again he found the connection blocked. "That little - just wait till I get hold of Inge."

The next number Hector tried was his old direct line. After his lawyer, the next best chance was his son. The call connected in seconds and Jeremy stared at him with a wooden smile.

"Thank god you're there. Get hold of that stupid lawyer of mine right away. He needs to straighten out this mess. You wouldn't believe everything that's happened-"

"Yeah, sure errrr... Dad. I mean, it's good seeing you. You must be having a blast."

"That's not what I..." Hector didn't have time to explain. "It's not like they said."

"No? It must be fun not worrying about things anymore." Jeremy glanced at his watch. "Look... 'Dad'. It's been... great... yeah, great, talking but I have a conference call with... someone. It's business, you know how it is..."

Something in Jeremy's face made Hector suspicious. His instincts kicked him firmly in the gut. Something was wrong; what could possibly be more important than a call from him? "Who's the call with, son?"

"Oh, it's not important Dad, just business. Don't worry about that stuff anymore. You go enjoy yourself."

Enjoy himself? Hector grimaced at what it had cost him to be able to make a call. "Listen Jeremy, I need you to pay attention. Something went wrong when I transferred. I've got no clothes, no money, no status. Everything I signed up for is gone. I'm telling you, son, I've been ripped off."

"Mr. Spagley on line three, Mr. Tren-Hump," announced Jeremy's desk phone.

"You're talking to Spagley? From the Union? Listen, son. Don't let those radicals push you around. Stall them if you have to and I'll take care of them once this mess is sorted out. Now get hold of Inge and tell him-"

"Sure Dad. Got to go. Been errr... great talking. Must do it again. Soon. Bye."

"Wait-"

The image vanished before Hector could say anymore. That worthless... after all he'd done for that ungrateful brat. The best schools, a Porsche on his 18th, Ferrari on his 21st. How many other kids had their own ten-meter yacht before they were twenty? And Hector knew all about the "secret" parties. He'd given that kid the best of everything. And now the idiot was going to let the unions walk all over him and destroy Hector's company.

Again his attempt to reconnect was blocked. The next number that came to mind was useless and Hector tried to avoid completing the call, but it connected automatically. He'd not spoken to Miley-Ellyn since she'd joined the commune as an "incubator" fifteen years ago.

"Hey, Dad. Good to hear from you. Been a long time. How are you?"

"Dead. Miley, I need you to get hold of my l-"

"Yeah? Cool. That's really cool. Aare you calling from Heaven?"

"Not exactly. I'm in Elyzium. You have to-"

"That's like… France huh? Is that where you died?"

Hector cursed. What had he ever done to deserve a daughter like this? Even the voluminous layers of material wrapped around her couldn't hide his daughter's state of extreme pregnancy and for a moment he forgot his circumstances. "How many is this?" he asked.

Miley-Ellyn looked confused momentarily, before cupping her burgeoning stomach with her hand and arm. "Oh this." Her brow furrowed. "This is hmmm… the seventh. Or maybe eighth. That's amazing, isn't it Dad? I brought all those small people into the world."

Hector felt the virtual veins in his head virtually throbbing, his temperature seeming to rise as though he'd explode any moment.

"From what the other women say, they think this one might even be free of venereal disease. There's a good chance that the Blessed Reverend Billy Paul may anoint me personally again soon. I just need to finish the course of antibiotics."

"Miley, something has gone wrong." Hector forced himself to be clear, knowing his time was running out. "I'm in Elyzium, but all my funds have been lost. I need you to contact my lawyer and get him on the case; they're trying to screw me over.

"Gee, I don't know Dad. I'd have to ask the Blessed Reverend Billy. And I don't know when I'll see him again."

A voice sounded and Miley looked around. "I have to go Dad. We're marching in support of the Workers Against Poverty. Gonna go right up to Tren-Hump Inc and blockade the entrance. Wow, I didn't know ghosts used phones like regular people, it's cool. Nice chatting, bye."

"You can't!" Hector snarled. This wasn't going how he'd expected. Didn't they understand how important he was? Without him they'd have had nothing. He still had some credit and thought a new number, though he had to admit it was a desperate choice. Kaydianne was decorative, but that was pretty much where her talents ended. He didn't expect an answer and was surprised when his wife picked up on the second ring.

"Hector? I didn't think... I mean this is like, totally unexpected." KayDianne was sitting on her bed wrapped in a pink fluffy towel. She'd redecorated; the bed and walls were pink too making her look like an adult living in a giant womb.

"Forget the small-talk, Babykins," Hector snapped. "I need you to contact Inge and tell him I've been screwed. He needs to go to LifePlus and force them to set up a call with me so we can talk properly."

KayDianne chewed on her lusciously enhanced lower lip. "Inge? Screw?"

Hector shook his head; KayDianne had met his lawyer dozens of times, but she wasn't the smartest. "My lawyer, you've met hi-"

"You want more already, you little fox?" A figure emerged from the bathroom wearing Hector's favorite G&D robe, the dark blue material making the man's skin looking even pastier than Hector remembered it.

"Inge?" Hector couldn't find the words. "KayDianne?" As he sat there open mouthed, the last few hard-earned seconds of his credit ticked away.

* * *

Hector pushed his way through the small crowd clustered around the hunt office. Several people slapped his back and he heard several mumbled "well done's." Even as he'd walked across town he'd heard several whistles and a couple of calls of "Go Hector!" It seemed news of his victory had spread fast.

Hector had never experienced any kind of adulation in his life. Of course, there was the usual sycophantic "Yes, sir" attitude of his underlings, but that wasn't genuine admiration. The response he got now though made him feel strangely warm and he even waved half-heartedly to some of the people calling out.

"Where were ya yesterday?" the ChaseMaster scowled.

"I…" Hector hesitated. He didn't see how he'd lost a day but nothing was quite how he expected it to be and he didn't feel comfortable enough to discuss the inconsistencies. "Well, that is…"

"No worries, son. Had to celebrate ya victory dincha?" The ChaseMaster grinned. "O'course now you'll see some real action."

"What do you mean?"

"You won. No one done that before. Ya not supposed to, see? The idea is, ya supposed to fight like a dog all the way and *lose*. Now everyone will want a piece of ya."

"Okay… I'll beat them too." Hector hoped he sounded more confident than he felt. "Anything new?"

"Couple of deals. Nothing you'd be interested in. Listen, you've got talent. If we work together, we can both do bonzer."

Hector had a plan of his own, but needed to expand his skills and an alliance with the ChaseMaster would be a vital component. The ChaseMaster was looking to line his own pockets of course, but Hector had plenty of experience manipulating people like that. "That's a good idea, we can help each other. What's available now?"

The ChaseMaster lifted an eyebrow. "Well, I've got one group that wants a medieval gig. Knights in armor, horses and all that malarkey. Weapons restricted to strict period availability, so we're talking lances, mace, swords. Pretty messy, I'd say."

Hector silently agreed. "The other?"

"Giant WarBots. Fully armored buggers. Ten meters high and equipped with everything going: miniguns, rockets, energy beams and full detection gear."

"That would be difficult; they'd need to pay big to make it interesting. I'd also need plenty of flight and invisibility to have even half a chance."

"Oh you'd get it. They quoted one kiloduck, a big fat one thousand shamoliens. With unlimited flight and invisibility for the duration."

Hector smiled.

"Ya don't get it." The ChaseMaster jabbed the screen. "They're setting up a custom game world to the east — all different zones: industrial, forest, ice, desert and anything else they can think of."

"They sound serious."

"They're creating a circus. And you'd be the star attraction. Your downfall will be the biggest event that ever happened in Elyzium. From what I hear it's even hit prime-time back in the world."

"I fooled them before."

"There'll be a dead zone around the home plate — a kilometer wide — where none of your skills will work. No flight, no invisibility, nothing."

Hector pulled back. "That's impossible."

"That's what I said." The ChaseMaster put his arm round Hector's narrow shoulders. "The way I see it, forget about these suicide runs and concentrate on high quality customers, people willing to pay for exclusivity. You've got a following, make the most of it."

"Tell them two kiloducks and they've got a deal. Fifty percent up front." Hector ran to the Judgment center and completed his assignments in record time. A thousand or two would be enough to make him pretty comfortable. But would it be enough to fight for what he'd been crewed out of? Ducks were currency in Elyzium but he doubted they'd get him legal help to fight his wife and slimy lawyer. It was tempting to take the money, but Hector knew sometimes it paid to wait for the payoff. His own plan would give him all that and more, but first of all he needed to visit the PimpDaddy again. All you need, he thought, is the right leverage…

The trees vanished abruptly as a fifteen meter section of forest splintered under the impact of a megawatt force beam, like a giant hand had slapped down on a patch of straw. Hector's eardrums seemed to implode and when he rubbed them his hand came away covered in red gore.

Bouncing upwards like a human sized flea he hopped several kilometers from the impact zone, streams of electric blue and red force beams intersecting with his path but not with him. Snapping on his invisibility, Hector jerked right mid-jump, hoping to evade any predictive weapons. He'd been on the hunt over four hours and had made almost no progress towards the target zone.

Touching down in soft yellow sand, Hector paused, dragging breath into his lungs in aching gasps. The dunes stretched endlessly in all directions, offering little in the way of cover. On the other hand it also meant there was little chance of him being caught unawares; he'd have seen the dust from one of those behemoths literally kilometers away.

Hector sat down heavily, his breath escaping in a low "oooff." He hadn't meant to sit down and in fact didn't want to, but the sand churned like liquid, providing nothing solid to stand on.

A giant head emerged from the sand, gleaming metallically in the bright desert sunshine, followed by shoulders and powerful mechanized arms. Hector lurched upright and ran obliquely left, away from the distinctive wind-up sound of the Bot's miniguns.

Bullets ripped a jagged path towards him and fire erupted throughout his entire body as a round caught his shoulder, tearing open the flesh and throwing him violently to one side.

Hector screamed, activating his invisibility by instinct as he scrabbled away. The firing stopped abruptly as the head of the Bot scanned from side to side like a blind turtle seeking a scrap of food. Blood coursed down Hector's arm and, even though he saw nothing, he could feel the warm streams dripping from the fingertips of his now paralyzed hand.

Two other WarBots joined in the search as Hector dragged himself over the crest of the nearest sand dune with his good hand, knowing just how vulnerable he was. Flight would undoubtedly trigger their motion trackers so he rolled over the next few dunes, hoping his body heat would be masked by the reflected heat.

The first Bot stopped scanning, edging along the path Hector had followed just moments before. It stopped repeatedly as if weighing up the situation. He was no threat, so there was some other explanation for the cautious behavior. Another drip left his fingers and Hector flinched. Whatever the Bot was tracking, its operator was struggling to follow the trail.

He checked the ground and saw nothing, but the Bot wouldn't have the same limitations. Hector could use this against them. Rolling to the bottom of the next sand dune he launched himself into the air away from the Bots. He moved in a straight line for several seconds to give them ample time to track him, before altering his path and zigzagging back and forth through the contours of the dunes.

Trails of machine gun rounds and laser beams streamed after him, throwing up waves of stinging particles that whipped at his eyes and skin. He dropped behind a particularly large dune knowing it would provide the shield he needed for the next part of his plan.

Looping back, Hector prayed his misdirection had been unnoticed. No weapons fire came his way and he tumbled in free fall towards the closest Bot. When he was less than a meter from its head, he plunged his fingers into his shoulder. Suppressing a scream he threw the invisible gore over the mechanized head and shoulders, making sure to liberally cover the missile packs.

Two more hops and Hector had dowsed the others. Rising upwards he switched off his invisibility again and waited for the inevitable…

Less than thirty seconds passed before the air around him was sliced apart by a raft of deadly beams. Ozone burned unpleasantly in his nostrils and he backed away at maximum speed. He spotted at least three rockets being launched — it was time to make an exit.

Reactivating his invisibility Hector jerked at random, but each move pulled him further from the missiles' detection radius.

The missiles hesitated as they struggled to track him. Hector smiled as they charged off in different directions. In the distance energy beam discharges flickered, but none came towards him and he was sure there was at least one large explosion.

The Palace was as deserted as ever, but this time held no fear as Hector slipped past the receptionist unseen. As before, the waiting room was empty and the door beckoned like a prize.

Hector was about to grab the handle but hesitated. The door had been locked before but even if it opened, it would have alarms and detectors to alert anyone inside. He wanted any meeting to be on his terms.

Hector retraced his steps and floated upwards, dropping onto a luxurious balcony seconds later. Wide French doors led inside and Hector strode through them. The VP sat behind a large mahogany desk surrounded by displays that filled the area with an ever changing cascade of light. The soft swell of cellos filled the air like a gentle stream.

Hector restored his visibility, his body flickering as it

reshaped itself. He looked down at the skin-tight dress and quivering large breasts hanging from his chest. The PimpDaddy had supplied just what he'd asked for — the right leverage, and sex always sells. Grabbing a large wine decanter, he stepped closer. "A drink, your worthiness?"

"Take a seat Tren-Hump, I'll be with you shortly." The VP glanced up. "And switch off that silly disguise please; the flickering is almost as annoying as you are."

Hector tried to project an air of confidence despite his shock. His appearance changed as he switched off the body he'd rented from the PimpDaddy and his breasts plopped onto the floor before evaporating in a twinkle of fairy dust. He looked around. With his experience of corporate excess he knew the room was more than just opulent.

Finally the VP looked up. "Drink? Glen Gilcullen isn't it?"

A glass appeared in Hector's hand.

"Don't be surprised. I've spent a lot of time studying your file. Far more than I should have in fact. I'm Granger by the way."

Hector lifted the glass and sipped the golden liquid, relishing the smooth warmth of the peaty alcohol as it teased his taste buds. Then the glass, contents and sensory input vanished.

"Everything is illusion here; you know that don't you?" Granger sipped his own drink and gestured expansively. "You, me, this room, the building... All a fake created by our volumetric imaging systems."

"How did you know it was me?" Hector asked, not touching the Whiskey that had reappeared.

"Do you see how clever it all is? It's so convincing that even people of obvious intelligence like you can't begin to understand it. You just had the illusion of feminine appearance. Identity in Elyzium isn't based on your projected Hoxels. If you came in here looking like a donkey, I'd still know it was you."

Hector grimaced at the word "donkey."

"Have you ever wondered why you can understand everyone? Every voice you hear is translated into whatever your brain pattern finds acceptable. It's like a computer game, except the players are all dead."

Granger laughed at Hector's puzzled expression. "I'm hooked up to all of Elyzium's servers; do you think for one second that there's something I'm not aware of if I want to be?"

"What you did in the game — that was so bad. Those people paid so much money for the environment, the WarBots." Granger waved his glass carelessly. "You know that they shot each other? Four hundred KiloDucks in damaged Hoxels there alone. Those rich people, like you used to be, eager to pay so much for a chance to slice you up. Now they're out of pocket and you're here."

"I won't cry for them," Hector said. "They wouldn't if the situation was reversed."

"Yes, what was it you used to say? 'Sentiment has no place in business.' Unfortunately you've become rather costly in a number of ways. Everything comes down to cost versus benefit — I'm sure you'd agree."

"My wife and lawyer-"

"Implemented a post-mortem financial adjustment on your Select agreement in line with the terms defined in Section 177, Sub-section 5, Paragraph 3."

Hector frowned. "I don't remember…"

"In so far that LifePlus shall attempt to comply with the wishes of the deceased, the company shall at no time be accountable for changes made through legal means employed by surviving relatives, creditors or government agencies in alignment with U.N. charter 170435: The Rights and Obligations to, and of, Virtual Personalities not maintaining a functional biological shell."

"It's quite a tragedy. Many of our clients Ascend only to find that their preservation isn't quite as important to their beloved survivors as it is to them. It's all legal and in good faith of course, the dead have no rights."

"That's not true. I remember some of that Charter." Hector didn't think it was worth mentioning that he only remembered it because he'd ridiculed it. "As part of your license you have to provide basic humane levels of interaction and activities for the personalities in your care. You can't just exploit us."

"You're familiar with the Judgment center…"

"Reinstate my original agreement and watch my 'cost' plummet," Hector blurted.

"What would I tell the shareholders? That I handed out thousands of Ducks on a whim? That I traded it to stop a minor annoyance?"

"The Ducks don't cost you anything. As you said 'it's all an illusion'"

"But even illusions need maintenance. If I gave you what you want then you'd no longer be a revenue stream. Didn't you once say that if you're not the one paying, you're the one getting sold?" Granger reached over and activated a single display. "There's this too."

Inge's narrow features appeared. "I have a restraining order." He smiled humorlessly. "Duly issued under Article 17, sub para 5, against the Entity known as Hector Tren-Hump, maintained on the Elyzium servers by LifePlus Inc. Effective immediately, said Entity must make no contact with any member of the living Tren-Hump family, employees of Tren-Hump Associates Inc. or the corporation's legal counsel, Travis-Inge-Badouil. Failure to comply will result in a motion to move said Entity to dormancy and possible complete termination for Digital Harassment. In addition, if the requested action is not taken, we shall be enacting compensation claims against LifePlus Inc, Life Counseling Services, Better Dead than Dead inc., Virtual Intelligence Systems and all other associated business entities."

"So you see Hector," Granger peered down his long nose, "You're *far* too expensive to ask for special treatment."

"There's no basis for accusing me of harassment. I'm legally entitled to make communications as I please."

"You are. But I can do this."

Hector saw Granger touch the display and his world turned gray. It was a strange shade that he struggled to recognize: bright, but not stimulating enough to be called "light." In fact he wasn't even sure it was gray; sometimes it seemed almost green, other times nearly black as his awareness changed.

As his eyes struggled to take in his new surroundings, he saw the swirling patterns that were usually the result of rubbing your eyes. It was maddening; something would appear to loom up in the corner of his vision but would melt away at any attempt to focus on it.

Worse, ants or spiders seemed to be crawling all over Hector's skin. When he tried to look at his arms and legs he realized he couldn't see himself. Was he blind? There was no sensation, not even the internal sense telling him the position of his limbs, or even if they existed. Just ants crawling over him, each tiny footfall bringing an electric shock of nerve stimulation in never ending waves of nausea.

Not just *on* his skin, underneath it too. They were inside him. Swarming inside him. Crawling inside his nose and ears. Scurrying inside his mouth and down his throat making him retch. Not ants, indescribable *things* that stung and bit and hopped and crawled. Slipping through the pores of his skin. Worming down hair follicles that somehow reached to his very core.

Hector tried to scratch everywhere, but had nothing to scratch with. The *things* crawled behind his eyes, into his brain and he screamed noiselessly.

Something slammed in to the back of Hector's head repeatedly as a painful white light burned through his tightly clenched eyelids. Squirming away from the light, he realized it was the floor hitting him as he jerked in trembling spasms like a dying fish.

```
Tren-Hump, Hector. TH15D3AD-1485-13A6-5661A946B3101857
Cycles: 265        CPU Credit: 1%        Ducks: 0.0
*MAIL*
```

Teeth grinding at his lack of Ducks, Hector activated the message.

"The Human Neural Network is such a fascinating thing, don't you think?" Granger's smooth voice sounded inside Hector's head. "LifePlus' technicians have done so much research on it and even they can't explain everything. It thrives on constant input stimuli, to such an extent that it starts to manufacture its own when deprived of them."

"Even the slightest variation of nothing becomes magnified and distorted, degenerating into a positive feedback loop that brings delusions and delirium. The result is an interesting descent into madness in a short period of time."

"I *know* you won't want to repeat the experience. The good news is, you don't have to. It's a choice you make."

The message cut off abruptly and Hector heard a familiar bellow in the distance.

"Prepare for Judgment. Prepare for Judgment. Come on Noobs. Move your lazy carcasses!"

Hector heard the snap of the whip and dragged himself to join the doleful line-up. No-one was cheering him now. All too soon he was back at a gray desk, swiping the controls to process the inane scenes that appeared.

The day seemed even longer than ever and Hector wondered about that. He'd dismissed it as the familiar illusion brought on by tedium, but was it that simple? LifePlus controlled everything; that much was certain. His perception of time didn't match with the reactions from his family.

If the company was manipulating mortizens' sense of time there must be a reason, but then Hector's speculations fell apart. What would be the point? He slapped a few invisible controls and directed the character on screen to choose the red ball and go left. "This is just stupid. What point is there to any of this?"

"Ain't that the truth? Like I said, that's why they call it work, bud."

"Fairy godmother?" Hector remembered the voice.

"Do you have any idea how much trouble you've caused?" The words hissed from an adjacent cubicle. "I doubt it. People like you don't care who they trample on. Every Mortizen who had contact with you or supported you has been given the third degree and had their Ducks confiscated. I can't have a virtual dump now without someone recording it."

"But why?"

"You threatened their business. Why else?" The voice paused. "You of all people should know that, Mister high-and-necking-mighty Tren-Hump. I thought maybe what happened might change you. People started to believe in you. I even put a necking bet on you myself. Five whole ducks. But all the while you we're just thinking about yourself."

"You know who I am?"

"I couldn't forget that voice after what *you* did. I was there. One of the miserable thousands you destroyed."

"You? But how…"

"I can understand your surprise. After I lost my job, I lost everything. First my friends left, then my wife and even my kids. I hit rock bottom, all thanks to you."

"You must have gotten back on your feet though, to get here I mean. Every cloud and so on."

The laugh was short and bitter. "That lottery ticket just blew me away. Who could have guessed? One piece of good luck in my life and what do I win? Millions of bucks? A Hollywood lifestyle? A mansion? Nope. I go and win free Ascendance."

Hector felt simultaneously embarrassed and resentful. "Why did you help me?"

"Oh I thought about doing something nasty to you. It used to keep me going through the day as I did these stupid games. But when you showed up, I didn't need to do anything. The worst thing you can do to someone used to privilege is take it away from them and they already had. Now you're just one of the chumps."

"I can do it again," Hector snapped.

"You hear that a lot around here." The faceless voice chuckled. "But every day the Marshals bring 'em in by the thousand."

"Thousand?" Hector stopped operating the controls.

"Over twenty thousand last I heard. And ninety percent of them are schmucks doing this."

Hector heard the slap of a hand on a desk float over the partition. If only a few percent were privileged, what were the rest doing? The answer was all too obvious — Judgment. But why?

It had to be more than just occupational therapy for the masses. Dead or alive, business didn't change and for LifePlus to invest so much into this they had to be making a profit from it, but how? One thing was clear: the majority of people didn't Ascend to a life, or death, of luxury. Granger's words jangled — who was being sold here? "What did you do before you were dead?"

The fairy godmother hesitated before answering. "I managed process control systems. Until bastards like you decided computers didn't need anyone watching over 'em."

That didn't help Hector. A computer was just a computer. Except... "What are computers bad at?"

"Are you kidding me?" The voice went quiet briefly. "Computers ain't smart. They never have been. Despite throwing massive amounts of SeePeeYoo and programming at them for decades — they're still just as dumb as always. Even the most advanced one don't got any smarts."

Hector thumped the control surface. That was it! Hector had invested in enough tech companies to know that they'd never managed to build a *real* artificial intelligence. It had always seemed obvious to him and he couldn't understand how the engineers couldn't see it — how could something with no experience of what it was to be human possibly ever think like one? LifePlus was selling the one thing computers couldn't provide, but something the Mortizens could: Judgment.

The Judgments were coded problems; real world scenarios wrapped up into individual packets of information with thousands of human intelligences ignorantly working out the answers; a giant multi-core human brain. "We have to hit them where it hurts," Hector whispered.

"Bah... what can we do?"

"I know how they operate. How the whole system works. I've years of experience — even they can't take that away and I can use it against them just as easily." Hector hammered his fist against the work surface. A word bounced around inside his head until he felt dizzy. It was crazy — an alien concept that only now made sense. "Spread the word. Everyone knows I can beat them. This time *we'll* beat them."

"What word?"

"Strike!"

The End

Dead Reckoning came out of nowhere really. I've read lots of stories about mind transfer and digital personalities and started to think about how that might work and who would have access to such technology if it became available. Surely the rich would be the primary beneficiaries, they'd be the people who could afford it and the ones most likely to believe they were worth preserving.

Throw in my fascination with computer games and "digital communities" and "Hector" was born. His name was chosen because that was what I intended to do to him throughout the story - put him through hell. It was almost irresistible making his situation worse and worse and ever more embarrassing. He's such a miserable, selfish old bastard that he deserves everything he gets, but strangely I found myself growing quite fond of him.

I had a lot more ideas that I could have included, but the story was already pretty long for a "short." I think it's safe to say that Hector will return at some point.

How Much Is That Doggy?

"Dad, you know it's for the best, don't you?"

Earl Duarte didn't know any such thing. His daughter had raised the suggestion of him going to live at the hideous-sounding "Sunset Dayz" more times than he wanted to remember over the last few years but he had no intention of giving in. He could just tell her that it was pointless now, but then he'd have to explain why and that would only cause more upset and anguish.

"We've discussed this Ellen. I'm used to having my freedom," His once-pleasant baritone voice had a soft rasp that he tried not to let sound like a growl. "I wouldn't be happy there."

"How do you know that? You haven't even looked at the brochures. They can take care of you, make sure you take your medications, and there'd be people to talk to. Not to mention how much easier it would be on me and the family. And how long is it since Steve visited?"

It always came down to the same emotional pressure: Do as you're told, Dad. Give us a break, Dad. It's funny When your kids are young, they depend on you, Earl thought; when they grow up you're re-cast as a feeble, half-witted encumbrance. As for Steve? Earl knew his son didn't come around anymore after a run-in with some of the local guys, but he wasn't going to share that fact with his daughter.

Ellen didn't let up: "You know you struggle here on your own. I have to fetch your groceries; the nearest store is over a mile away. I have nightmares about you having a fall. And I can't be around all the time. We have lives too."

"I get by. I always have." Earl smiled, rubbing ineffectually at the brown spots on the back of his hands. "I haven't needed anyone to look after me in a whole heap of years."

"And what if something happens? This isn't a good neighborhood anymore. Most of the people who lived here when we were kids are gone and the people who've moved in…" Ellen pulled a face. "They look more like squatters than home owners. And what about your kidneys? If I can't drive you, you have to struggle half-way across town to the clinic. The temperatures are dropping now fall is setting in; you might catch a chill or something."

He had to admit that was true. When he'd started feeling weak, Earl had reluctantly agreed to visit the clinic, knowing full well it wouldn't be good news. There were growths on his kidneys, requiring another addition to the never-ending series of pills and potions he'd gradually acquired as part of his daily diet.

Dr. Makram had gone overboard of course; stubborn patients like Earl didn't come in every day, so they'd taken the opportunity to run a whole series of tests. Luckily, Ellen hadn't been party to it all and he'd "forgotten" to mention the problems they'd found with his eyesight and signs of degenerative Alzheimer's. Why worry her and the grandkids? It wasn't as if they could do anything anyway.

Except perhaps, put him in a home.

"Look, Ellen. I've taken care of myself since I was fourteen and your grandparents passed away. I managed to live through the war. I survived the Uranium mines. I looked after myself when your mother was alive and I've managed just fine since she died. I see no reason to change that now."

"But Dad…" Ellen seemed to sense she'd lost the battle again. "Look, regardless of anything else you get lonely here. You know you do. At 'Sunset' you'd have lots of friends, people your own age who share your interests."

"I don't need friends. All I want is peace, Ellen. Can't you give me that one small thing?" He didn't want to watch people die and didn't want them watching him either. Earl gestured towards the window, where the craggy, black outline of the Grand Mesa dominated the skyline like an ever-present approaching thunder storm. "I spent most of my life underneath that thing, Ellen. It comforts me being able to see it from up here now."

Of course, they used to have friends, lots of friends. Isobel used to love entertaining and he'd been happy to indulge her. Even if he hadn't enjoyed the parties, he'd have put up with them just to see her smile. Her whole face would glow like the sun on a warm spring day.

Bel had even put up with his beer buddies, including old Rafakat who quite honestly was a pain in the butt. Rafakat was always telling everyone how Earl had saved his life in the mines. But it wasn't like it was anything heroic; Earl had simply pushed the strange little guy out of the way by instinct when the roof came in and that was the end of it. But that didn't stop Rafakat from taking every opportunity to tell the tale, each time grander than the last and always finishing the same way: Earl saved my life-someday I'll make it up to him. And if that wasn't embarrassing enough, Rafakat was also partial to every crazy notion going and would happily prattle about them for hours .

Earl had often wondered how Rafakat ended up working in the mines. He never seemed to quite belong and talk about clumsy. There wasn't a single piece of equipment that Rafakat hadn't tripped over at one time or another.

What kind of name was that anyway? Rafakat? Earl had asked once, but the man had just smiled. It sounded foreign, Asian or middle-eastern maybe; and certainly the man had a light, coffee-colored skin that supported that idea. Earl couldn't even remember if his old co-worker had ever used a first name -or maybe Rafakat *was* his first name. The memory was lost in one of the "fuzzy areas" Earl tried to ignore.

"Dad? Are you okay?" Ellen eyed him closely.

"What? Yeah, sure. Sorry hon, I was just thinking about old times." Earl patted Ellen's hand. "I know you're worried for me but really, I'm doing okay."

"You're lonely, Dad. What kind of daughter would let you sit here turning to dust like everything else in this place." She waved a hand at the bric-a-brac that overflowed every shelf and drawer.

Earl sighed. "It was your mother's, you know that. It's all I have left of her, other than memories." It was more than the remnants of Bel's life. A home isn't just something that starts and stops with things, it's like a shrine to the experiences of those who live in it. But Earl knew he couldn't explain that.

"Well, it's your choice. But I'm not going to just let things drop, Dad."

Earl had to smile; at times like these he knew for sure that Ellen was completely legitimate - she had exactly his kind of stubborn.

Ellen was busy for the next few days—something Earl wasn't too unhappy about. The clinic had contacted him again; the last test was worse than anticipated. His kidneys were degenerating more rapidly than initially thought and "we're very sorry Mister Duarte to give you such bad news. If there's anything else we can do please feel free to…"

Well, at least now I don't have to worry about the dementia, Earl thought.

A quiet noise drew his attention to the door. "Probably just kids," Earl muttered. Then it sounded again, a scratching followed by several squeaks.

Earl dragged himself out of the chair and shuffled to the door, cursing under his breath. His aching joints seemed worse every day and the deeper pain in his kidneys made almost every move a battle. He peered through the peephole, the ancient lens muddying the view almost to the point of uselessness. For a second he thought he saw the shadow of a man outside, then he blinked and it was gone.

Again a light scraping noise accompanied by a sad mewl.

Earl opened the door a few inches, but it was wrenched from his hand. A dark blur shot past his feet and he staggered backwards. He closed the door and turned. A small coffee-colored dog sat in the center of his living room, its tongue lolling out of the side of its mouth in a way that even the hardest of souls would have to describe as "cute."

"Hey, you can't stay here puppy. Go on. Shoo!"

Earl reached toward the door, but the dog had other ideas. He ran—or rather bounced—around the room several times, tripping over just about everything possible.

Earl didn't stand a chance of catching the animal and sat back down. Finally, the dog stopped and looked up at him with big dark eyes and yelped. The little tail beat a frantic tattoo on the floor before it launched itself onto the old man's lap. Paws that seemed far too big for it pressed against Earl's chest as it gifted his face with licks.

"Where are you from little fella? You can't stay here you know. I don't have anything for you."

Earl searched the dog for a collar and tags, but there was nothing. "Come on, let me put you back outside. You need to get yourself home."

The dog jumped down and backed into the farthest corner, front paws clamped over its ears and eyes as it squeaked tragically. Earl looked out at the fading light and could almost feel the autumnal evening chill creeping inside the house. It was the time of year to snuggle up in cozy warmth, not be exposed to the elements, especially for a puppy.

"Okay. You can stay, but only until Ellen comes and can take you to a shelter."

The puppy exploded in a fury of yelping, bouncing and tail

wagging. The dog reminded Earl of someone, but he couldn't put his finger on who.

"A dog?" Ellen peered around the room, chewing her lower lip. "You're not thinking of keeping it?"

"Well, I wasn't at first." Earl smiled as the puppy rolled head-over-paws from behind the couch. "But, to be honest, he makes me feel better. You keep telling me I need some company."

"People to look after you, not a dog to burden your life and what if…" Ellen hesitated. "I mean, if something happens don't expect me to look after it."

Earl knew Ellen was right. He didn't need a dog that would outlive him by years to complicate his life, but the few days since the dog had arrived had been the best he'd had in a long time.

"Look, hon. I know it's hard to understand, but I just want him around. If it doesn't work out we can take him to the shelter. They'll look after him."

"Dad, you're the one who needs looking after. If you'd look at the brochures, I'm sure you'd-"

"I'm not discussing that again, Ellen. I've told you before, I'm not leaving. This is my home." Earl scratched at the spots on his hands. He'd raised his family there. Every corner overflowed with amber memories of laughing children, joyful smiles and the occasional tears. Of course the house was too big for him on his own, but what did that matter? It was like an old sweater, worn and frayed, but fashioned by the years to a perfect fit. Giving it up would be like giving up on his whole life. He wanted to die surrounded by those memories, not by people examining him and prodding him and watching him, but no way could he explain that to Ellen.

"I understand that you're a mean, selfish old fool who doesn't know what's good for him, or when someone is trying their best to help."

The dog yelped.

"He must agree with you." Earl reached out and squeezed Ellen's hand, ignoring the pain it caused in his fingers. "You win. I'll look at the damn things."

Ellen looked close to tears. "Don't keep him, Dad. If you do decide to move, it will only make things harder." She eyed the puppy suspiciously. "And we certainly couldn't take him in, if that's what you're thinking. The brochures don't show the whole story, I could arrange a visit to 'Sunset', so you could see it for yourself."

"I said I'd look at them, Ellen. Don't push it."

Ellen hesitated as though she was going to say something else, but changed her mind. "Well, you have to give him a name if you're keeping him. What's it going to be?"

Earl smiled as the puppy wrestled heroically with the corner of a curtain. Then its grip loosened and it slipped backwards to tumble once more over one of his shoes. "I'll call him Kat."

"Oh don't be silly Dad. You can't call a dog 'Cat'."

"Not C-A-T." Earl reached down and roughed the back of the puppy's head. "K-A-T."

"Kat? Come on, you can think of something better."

"What do you think boy?" Earl patted his knee and the pup hopped up, rubbing its damp black nose against his. "Kat?"

Yrraap!

"Well, you two seem to have settled that." Ellen stood up. "I have to make tracks."

"I need to run to the store. I'll need some feed and bowls and a bed of some kind."

Ellen frowned and her lips whitened. "You're not running anywhere and it's getting dark."

"I'll cope."

"I can be there and back in twenty minutes."

Earl wanted to object, but didn't relish the thought of walking all that way and trying to carry such bulky items back. "Thanks, Hon."

The next few weeks smeared from one to the next, almost without a break. Earl's usual routine had dragged with an old clock's weary ticking. The flash of days and weeks is the privilege of the young, he thought, while the elderly are forced to suffer each decline, minute by ponderous minute.

Now Kat had changed all that. The little pup was a singular burst of energy, immune to any kind of senescent inertia, dragging Earl along for the ride.

It wasn't just that Earl was now responsible for making sure Kat got enough exercise; he truly enjoyed taking the dog out and playing with him. Once again a walk in the park became an adventure and a stroll along the beach was entertainment for an entire day.

Wrapped up so much in Kat's clowning, Earl almost forgot his stiffness and ever-present kidney pain. Even his vision seemed to be clearer, leaving him the simple pleasure of watching the little dog wringing the most out of each moment.

Even trips to the clinic couldn't separate them. Earl insisted on keeping Kat with him, playing on the staff's weaknesses until they indulged him with soft reproachful clucking.

"Well, we don't normally allow pets in the surgery… but in this case Mr. Duarte, I have to say that this little friend of yours seems to have had a beneficial effect on you." Dr. Makram patted Kat's head. "The tests show the degeneration in your kidneys appears to have stabilized. At least for now."

"From having a dog?"

"Presumably you're getting out more to exercise the little fellow and that's helping you too."

"What about the rest of me?" Earl decided to ask, even though he knew what the answer would be.

"Let's see." Makram pored over the other results, not saying anything for several minutes. "Hmmm, that's a little odd—your white cell count is down and the MRI shows that the atrophy in your cortical tissues has slowed."

Earl could guess what "odd" meant: nothing good that was for sure. "It's okay, Doc. I didn't expect anything else."

"What?" The Doctor's thoughts were elsewhere. "No, don't misunderstand. White cell count is a general indicator of disease, so lowering means less infection and the declining atrophy means that your brain structure isn't degenerating as rapidly as we feared it might. All in all these are good signs. It's just a little surprising considering the earlier tests."

"That can't be related to Kat?" Earl scratched at a dark patch on his skin. "Can it?"

"Cat? Oh, your puppy. No, it's just the way of these things, Mr. Duarte. Sometimes they're active and progress quickly and then other times they can almost slip away to the point of not being there. We don't really understand why."

Earl didn't care. It was good news and he needed that right now. It's not easy to watch yourself slowly deteriorate, your own body start to fight against you. Whatever the reason, it was good to see the downhill stretch level off, even if it was temporary.

He could feel it too. Ever since Kat had appeared, life had changed: he felt more alert, more energetic. Whether that was purely psychosomatic, he didn't know. He felt better than he had in years, and that was all that mattered.

Earl came out of the bedroom and looked around. Normally Kat was up and waiting for him as soon as he woke, but today there was no sign.

"Kat? You there, boy?"

Earl caught the faintest of sad whines from the back of the sofa and edged past the piles of dusty books to look. Kat was stretched out, panting heavily and occasionally nipping at his side with his teeth, the chewed fur matted and wet.

"What is it Kat? What's wrong?"

Earl knelt, his knees creaking in protest. The dog looked up at him and mewled softly. Tears formed in the old man's eyes as he stroked Kat, gently whispering words of comfort.

"It'll be okay, boy. Hang in there. It'll be okay." Dragging himself upright, Earl picked up the phone.

"Ellen. I need help. Now…" The words came out in a tumble. "It's Kat."

"Dad? What's wrong?"

"Kat's hurt. I need help." That was all that seemed to matter.

Ellen hesitated. "Dad, sorry I'm just heading out to drop off the girls. I'm sure he'll be alright. Look, I'll come over later on, okay?"

Earl banged the phone down and hurried to the bedroom, coming back with one of his blankets to wrap around the puppy. He needed a vet. There was one down on Lee—he remembered seeing the sign—but that was a long walk for him: nearly three miles.

It didn't matter.

Cradling Kat in his arms, Earl set off down the street. The sun was up and it was already getting unseasonably warm despite the morning frost. But he had no thoughts for the pleasantness of the day. Kat needed help. Half an hour later though, he was sweating with the effort. A silver flash in the road caught his peripheral vision, but he ignored it.

"Dad!"

Earl turned. "Ellen?"

"I knew you'd try something stupid. Why couldn't you wait? And where's your coat?"

"I wasn't thinking. Kat's sick. He needs help." Earl realized how feeble it sounded.

"Get in. You'll have a stroke if you're not careful."

Earl sat rubbing his hands together. The vet was taking his time examining Kat. It would have been better if Ellen had stayed, but she had to work and had left him with strict instructions to call a cab for the journey home, something he'd have done earlier if he hadn't panicked.

"Mr. Duarte?" The vet emerged at long last. "I've finished my examination. He's going to be fine."

Earl stood up. "Are you sure? What's wrong with him?"

"Well, he has an infection and from the tests it looks like he has some problems with his kidney functioning. We've given him a shot and a few antibiotics will take care of the rest. I'm sure you'll quickly see a big improvement."

"Kidney problems?" Earl swallowed hard.

"Yes. Nothing serious at this stage but we'd like to monitor him if that's possible. You should schedule some regular visits if you don't mind."

"No… that is, sure. Anything I can do for the little guy."

"You had me confused." The vet smiled. "From what you said when you brought him in, I was expecting a much younger animal."

"Younger? But he's only…"

"I understand. They grow up so fast." The vet offered Earl a box of pills. "Give him one of these twice a day and things will be okay. I suggest bringing him back in three months for a check; if you don't see any change in two weeks bring him back anyway."

The door into the examination room opened and a young girl led out a rather sad looking Kat.

"Let's get you home, Kat." Earl smiled at the girl. "Would you call a cab for me please?"

He didn't mention that Kat looked almost twice as old as the last time Earl had looked at him closely. And that was just the previous night.

Back home, Earl wrapped Kat in the blanket and watched as the dog rested, listening to Kat's soft panting.

"What the hell is going on here, Kat?"

Earl's voice was soft, but Kat still flicked up one floppy ear and whimpered at the sound of his name, his dark eyes never leaving Earl.

"Whatever it is, I don't think I like it."

Kat improved considerably with the help of the antibiotics and in a few days Earl felt happy to resume their earlier routine of walks in the park and along the beach. Kat seemed happy and had returned almost to his former self. Despite his appearance, the dog still enjoyed clowning around like a puppy.

The truth was though, Kat no longer resembled a puppy. His coat had gotten wiry and he'd lost much of the juvenile pudginess that had been obvious just a few weeks ago. In fact, Earl thought he could see a touch of white around the dog's muzzle, and that definitely hadn't been there earlier.

"Here you go boy." Kat hopped onto Earl's lap, eager to devour the offered treat before settling down across the man's knees. "I wish you could tell me what's happening."

"Did I tell you that Ellen's coming?" Earl's hand moved across the dog's back in gentle strokes. "She's bringing the children too; haven't seen them in way too long."

Earl opened up the letter from the clinic, only glancing at the note inside. He wasn't interested in what they had to say anymore. He was doing okay and feeling fine. What did they know about things anyway, with all their tests and theories? He felt healthy. Who could argue with that?

Earl rubbed the back of the dog's ears, eliciting contented growls. "All that matters is how we feel, isn't it?"

Yrrrapp!

"They'll be here soon. We can have some lunch; I got some cake in especially for the girls. And after that we can take them for a walk in the park. You'd like that wouldn't–" Earl stopped stroking, eyes transfixed on the back of his hand. It couldn't be. That was impossible.

The skin on his hands was a smooth and even pink—not a trace of a spot anywhere.

Earl slid Kat onto the floor, hurried to the large mirror over the bathroom sink and peered into its misty reflection. Moving in slow motion, he lifted the cloth to the glass and wiped away the dust, mesmerized by the sight that greeted him.

The reflection was his, but it was a reflection he hadn't seen in over twenty-five years.

The puffiness was gone from under his eyes, the wrinkles

and spots had faded away and his hair was showing dark with just a few hints of gray at the temples. What was more, he realized with a shock, he could actually see himself clearly. He'd stopped wiping the mirror years before, partly because he didn't like to watch the seemingly daily deterioration, but also because his failing eyesight made it a pointless exercise.

This was... Earl found he didn't have any words for it; instead he rushed back into the living room and grabbed the paper. Not stopping to put on his glasses, he turned to the back pages and read aloud. "Sports car champion, Henry Yong, made an impressive debut in the Champ Car World Series with a top-six finish at the Grand Prix of America in his first race..."

It had been ten years since Earl had been able to read anything other than the large print headlines without his glasses. He flicked to check another page in disbelief, but at that moment the creak of the door announced Ellen's arrival.

"Hi Dad. Sorry, we're a little—"

"Hi Hon. Hi girls." Earl opened his arms wide. "How about a hug for your old gramps?"

Neither Ellen nor the girls moved.

"Dad?" Ellen edged forward, her hand close to her mouth. "What's happened?"

"Happened? Well, nothing. I mean, well I don't know. It's like a miracle or something."

"What is that? Make-up?" Ellen gazed at him, still keeping her distance. "Did you dye your hair?"

Earl laughed. "I didn't do anything. It's me. Just me."

"But Dad..."

"Never mind, come and give your old man a squeeze. You too, girls."

Lunch was subdued. Ellen and the girls said little as they ate. Earl felt the sidelong glances when they thought he wasn't looking. Even the cake didn't produce more than a quiet "thank you" from his granddaughters. Things eased a little as the youngsters chased around the park with Kat, while Ellen sat with Earl on a sun-washed bench watching them play.

"What's going on, Dad?" Ellen's voice was quiet but intense. "And don't fob me off; I know when something isn't right."

Earl hesitated. "I'm not sure I understand it myself. All I know is that I feel alive like I haven't in years. You remember the parties we used to have? When all the family and friends used to come around?"

Ellen nodded.

"We had so much to live for then, your mom and me. You kids were young and life was sweet. It felt like nothing could ever change that."

"But things do change: we got older, I lost your Mom, you and Steve grew up. And there isn't anything you can do about it. That's the damnedest thing; inside you feel the same, but you're betrayed by your own body."

"And now?"

"Now?" Earl stopped. What about now? "Now I have what looks like a second chance, and nothing is going to stop me from taking that. Not you, not the girls, not anyone."

"But it's not right Dad, not natural... you–"

"Ellen?" She slid back slightly when he reached out to her. "Would you prefer I was still sick?"

"Of course not, how can you say such a thing. It's just-"

The air was rent by a pair of shrill screams. Both adults looked up to see the girls running towards them white-faced.

Ellen jumped up. "What is it? What's wrong?"

Nothing but incoherent sobs came from the two youngsters and as Earl went over to try and help he realized Kat was nowhere in sight.

Earl stopped and turned full circle. "Kat? Here boy."

"Take it easy girls. Talk to Mommy."

"Girls? Where's Kat?" Earl felt his stomach flip-flop. "Have you seen him anywhere?"

"Dad?" Ellen hissed. "They're upset and all you can think

about is your dog?"

"Here, Kat." Earl turned to the girls. "You were playing with him. What happened? Where is he?"

Without waiting for a reply, Earl jogged down the grass to where he'd last seen them together. Not even noticing the incongruity of his fluid movements. "Kat! Here boy. Come to Pops." He walked around a bank of withered roses, the scent of decay adding to the nauseous feeling in the pit of his stomach.

Kat lay unmoving on the grass.

Earl rushed up and cradled the dog in his arms. Kat's frame seemed to have shrunk, like there was too much fur or maybe not enough Kat to fill it properly. Earl stroked the dog's head hoping to get some sign of life out of him, but there was no response.

"What is it, Kat?" Earl's eyes stung as he forced back tears, lifting the dog carefully and carrying him back to Ellen and the girls.

"Dad?"

"I need your car keys, Ellen. He's hurt and I need to get him to the vet."

"You can't drive, Dad. They wouldn't renew your license—remember? I'll take you."

"Just give me the keys. I'll drop you on the way." Earl held out his hand and waited until Ellen fished inside her bag and handed them over.

The drive to the animal hospital was a blur. Afterward Earl couldn't have said whether the traffic was heavy or light; in fact he couldn't remember any of the journey at all. All he remembered was striding up the steps, holding Kat like the most prized treasure in creation.

"Please, you have to help him… like last time." Earl pleaded at the girl behind the desk. "Do something, I'm begging you."

Earl waited, his forehead pressed against the cold smoothness of the picture window that looked out onto the parking lot. He wondered again what had happened to him and Kat. He wasn't sure. All he knew was that when he thought about losing the little dog, a hole opened up inside him that felt like it would suck in his heart and soul.

A noise made Earl turn. The vet was grim-faced.

"I'm sorry Mr. Err…" He glanced at the card. "Mr. Duarte. It was too late, there was nothing we could do for the poor fellow."

"You mean?" Earl sank to his knees, burying his face in his hands.

"The nurse seemed to think that you'd brought the dog in recently, but that must be a mistake. I'd remember any dog as ill as that little chap."

"What was it?" Earl tried to stand but couldn't, finally propping himself up and dragging himself into a chair by the window.

"Well, as near as I could make out he had complete liver failure, complicated further by a number of age-induced infections. There's no way to be sure without a complete autopsy." The vet paused. "I'm sorry. You must have had him a long time."

"Since… he was a puppy." Earl sobbed.

"Of course." The vet turned.

"Wait." Earl called to the retreating figure. "Do you recognize me?"

The vet turned back. "Funny you should ask. The name's familiar, but I don't recognize you, I must admit. Have we met before?"

"I guess not."

Earl walked blindly out of the surgery to the car, too numb to think about where he was heading. He drove without thought, taking random turns for what must have been several hours, stopping only by instinct for red lights.

Weeks passed and Earl struggled on. He hadn't felt such loneliness since losing Isobel and now it seemed so much worse because of his own transformation. He still didn't understand what had happened and wasn't sure whether it had been a curse or a blessing, his physical improvement soured by the fact that his family had virtually disowned him.

He'd only seen his daughter twice since the park and she'd left the girls in the car both times. Ellen said they didn't want to see him anymore, but Earl hadn't believed that and pushed past her. When he'd opened the car door, the girls had screeched, huddling together white-faced at the far side of the seat. Earl backed away confused.

Today though, he needed a walk. Whether it was the unexpectedly bright sun or something else, he felt an urge to get out of the house. He stuffed his hands in his pockets and pulled the coat tight around him. Though sunny, the chill of winter filled the air as he strode through the streets.

By rights he should have felt grateful for what had happened. He'd been given a second chance, another opportunity to make the most of life, but it seemed empty. Bel was still gone; nothing he could do would change that. He'd wondered whether he should look for someone new, but just thinking about it brought a sour taste to his mouth. Now he'd lost Ellen and the grandkids too. He felt hollow, as if he'd stolen a life that didn't belong to him. Perhaps Ellen had been right; he really was a selfish old man. No matter how good he felt, he didn't want this if it cost him his family.

Passing a litter-strewn alley, a soft noise caught his attention. It was so quiet that by rights he shouldn't have heard it over the traffic. Earl moved down the lane, stopping frequently as he strained to locate the sound, eventually tracing it to a loose stack of wooden crates. Picking the jumble apart, he placed each shard to one side, finally revealing a shivering, bedraggled mass of damp fur. Dark button eyes looked up at him sadly from either side of a white-flecked nose.

"Who are you then, old fellow?" Earl ran his hand across the dog's head. "No collar, huh? You're too old to be out here on your own."

He slipped his coat off, no longer feeling the icy wind,

and wrapped it around the dog; cradling the animal against his chest. The dog looked wary, but soon settled into the crook of Earl's arms with a grateful murmur.

"Everything's going to be okay." Earl scratched the dog's ears softly, feeling a familiar twinge in his side. "I'll make it all right again. You'll see."

The End

Much has been published about the value of pet ownership. Pet owners tend to be more active, healthier, and better-balanced mentally. These ideas mixed with the fact that many religions believe in reincarnation, especially in the form of animals gave me this story. It was the first short I wrote in our new Canadian home and I felt a new found optimism about the future. I'd also lost my own dog Jake, a few months before we moved to Canada and still missed him deeply. Writing this story had a deeply cathartic effect and opened the way to us introducing another dog (Kyla) into our little family later in 2006. Tragically we lost Kyla too a few years ago and we've never been able to bring ourselves to get another dog. It's still hard for me to read this story without getting upset.

Dust to Dust

Shards of adobe ripped into Holbrook's face as the wall exploded next to him. He threw himself down; he hadn't even heard the rifle shot. Bitter dust-like sand filled his mouth, grinding between his teeth as if he were chewing on glass. The wind gusted and all he could see was sand, leaving him only a vague idea where the rest of his squad was.

"Norton? Fredricks? You there?"

No reply. Holbrook pressed down into the heat-soaked ground and crawled forwards, the baking sand sticking to his exposed skin. There was something barely visible through the swirling clouds. His stomach tightened thinking it was the body of one of his comrades, but it turned out to be the lip of one of the many shell-holes that pock-marked the Sudan desert. A hollow, metallic bark of an AKM cut through the wind and he rolled into the hole as bullets tore the edge apart.

"Dodged another one," he grunted.

He heard two soft thuds and span around. Grenades! Holbrook hurled himself back as the force of the blast seared his face.

Holbrook opened his eyes and saw an angel. At least if it wasn't an angel he had no idea what to call it. It floated in the air and its translucent body glowed as it moved around him as

73

if examining him from all sides.

You safe. Healthy.

He sensed the words impossibly inside his head, unsure if they were real.

"I'm alive?" He wasn't sure the angel would hear him.

We save you.

"Thanks." The word didn't seem enough. He felt okay though. There were no sensations of any wounds. "I'm glad you did."

Ones before not like. Want return immediately.

"I can go back?" Holbrook looked around; the space didn't look much like heaven, more like some kind of lab. He was surrounded by a number of box-like units lined with what appeared to be instruments of some sort, and two large cylinders dominated one corner reaching all the way up to the roof. He couldn't put names to any of it though. "Where is this? Who're you?"

This Joleran, homeworld. Three-thousand light years from your planet. I Preel, leader Project Savior.

Holbrook didn't believe in flying saucers or little green men. He shook his head; this couldn't be happening. I must be high on drugs or something, he thought. Maybe I'm in hospital, some kind of weird dream. If I lie here quietly, eventually they'll wake me up and-

Your senses function correctly. I answer questions.

Preel morphed. A thick extension of the creature's flesh reached out and molded against Holbrook's head. The tendril was cool against his forehead, then tingled, seeming to heat up until it burned. Thoughts flashed through his mind almost too quickly for him to follow. The Mechnas. War. Devastation. Decades. The Joles. Helpless. Pacifist. Unfamiliar with war and terror. Beaten. Retreat. Until only the homeworld remained. Last hope. Savior. Many attempts.

"The Mechnas are destroying you and you need help fighting them? I hate to disappoint you, but I'm just one guy, not Rambo."

You train we. We fight. We not good. Many years peace. You help us find again. Learn. Kill.

"Hell, that would take months. And I'm not even sure…" Holbrook rubbed the stubble forming on his jaw. "Look, I can't stay here that long; I've got a girl…"

Not months. Small time. Hours. We link your brain. Accelerated learning. Experience share. Please. Help.

There was a desperation to the thoughts Holbrook received, a terrible cry of pain and loss that spoke of years of struggle. If it was hours, he could rationalize it. They'd saved his life after all. He could spare that sort of time in return. He grinned when he thought about what the other guys would say when he got back. They'd be buying him beer for the rest of his tour.

Preel led Holbrook to a large capsule-shaped booth covered in fine pimples, like the surface of a golf-ball turned inside out, and shuffled him inside before he could object. Everything went dark and he blinked. Darkness was replaced by the sizzling heat of African Veld, the smell of hot grass sharp in his nose.

Holbrook shaded his eyes against the fierce glare of the sun and saw his arm daubed with gray mud. In one hand he held a long spear, in the other a leaf-shaped wooden shield. A shout of alarm. Men charged toward him and the village behind him. Sun blinding. Figures melting. Blurs flashed past his eyes. Like a movie frame melting. Ears buzzed. He sank to his knees clasping his head as the noise became a deafening scream.

Our apologies.

"I thought you wanted me to help, not try kill me." Holbrook cradled his head in his hands.

Your mind slow. Not anticipated. Pushed too much, too fast.

"You better just send me back." Holbrook had the mother of all hang-overs and didn't want to repeat the experience. "This isn't gonna work."

Nothing back there. Why you leave?

"*Everything* I have is there. I know you're compassionate. Your mind showed me when we err... 'linked.' Look, you *can* return me can't you?"

We can return. To origin. Place and time.

"Great. No one will know I was gone." He was starting to wonder if it might be better not to mention this. They might lock him up if he did.

You no future there. Here you live centuries. Your time.

"You're wrong." Holbrook pulled back. "There's a whole world waiting back on Earth."

We slow Accelerator. Training take days not hours. Preel paused momentarily. *Is acceptable?*

First Holbrook was a Roman Legionnaire, fighting barbarians in the northern lands. The Centurions with him died in seconds at the hands of blue-stained hordes. Next he led British troopers against mass charges of Zulu warriors. Then he was at the controls of a Flying Fortress over the fields of Europe, as waves of Luftwaffe Messerschmitts tore into the flanks of the unprotected squadron.

The scenarios were pulled out of his mind and each time the supporting Joles grew more skilled and confident. Initially it was as if they were in a daze. Now they acted like coordinated, tempered soldiers, killing efficiently and carrying the battle to the enemy. Holbrook was suffering though. Constantly fighting the ultra-realistic battles was even more stressful than real combat because of the infrequent breaks. He never had time to recover from one session before the next started.

Now he was part of a multi-being StarChaser, individuals coming together as one. Projected energy beams and force fields allowed them to tear through Mechna fleets and rout their attackers.

Holbrook gasped as he came out of the accelerator, his skin pale and drawn and his stomach hollow from being unable to fully digest the nourishment the Joles provided. The Joles also found that something in the dust on the planet was reacting with his lung membrane, resulting in a caustic bronchial irritation and making him fight for each breath.

Our scientists are working on better food. It won't be long. Preel's thoughts had grown more fluid as their association had developed, increasingly coming across like regular English to Holbrook.

"That *has* to be enough. I can't take any more."

Preel came over and extruded a tentacle to brush Holbrook's head softly. At some point Holbrook had realized that Preel wasn't exactly male, and maybe not exactly female either. The touch soothed him as it always did, but this time it wasn't enough; he felt like his mind was disintegrating slowly the longer he stayed. One more battle and he'd lose it completely.

"Send me home, please." he croaked.

Your life is here. Your future here.

"No! I've done all I can."

Preel hesitated before answering; its voice tinged with sadness. *It is enough. Our people will defeat the Mechna now. But stay with us. You are hero. We celebrate and reward for your help.*

"I just wanna go home. I *need* to go home. You said you could send me back." The words tripped out almost in a babble. "Tell me you didn't lie."

We don't lie.

"Then do it."

Preel pressed Holbrook down until he was lying flat on the platform, still stroking his forehead. Another extrusion moved to a nearby instrument panel.

I send you back. I'm sorry, Holbrook. I hoped you would learn to like it here, with me.

"Don't be sorry. I'm glad I could help." A flood of sadness washed through Holbrook as Preel's emotions touched him directly. "Please understand. I need to be with my own kind."

Preel pressed the box.

Farewell, Holbrook. You will not be forgotten. Return to your place and time.

Holbrook felt nothing for the smallest instant. Then the oppressive heat of sand-filled air hit him from all sides and he tasted the bitter dust of the desert. Two gentle thuds sounded in the sand and he looked around.

Grenades...

The End

Dust To Dust had a strange origin. I'd been thinking about writing something about a soldier teaching an alien race how to fight for a while but hadn't quite managed to work out the overall framework and plot. Then one day I was reading about "flash fiction" and wondered if I could write something that short (I tend to be a little more wordy!). Somehow the two ideas came together and so I dashed out the first scene and part of the second. I went to sleep that night and when I woke I had the whole idea fully formed in my head. I sat down immediately and wrote it out before I forgot anything!

Murphy's Law

IT appeared sometime in August and the world plus canine friends completely failed to notice. The first indication came from a BioSat that reported a complete shutdown of Earth's ecosystems. Obviously that never happened.

No one saw the implications. Some backroom technician noted that number seventeen BioSat had "anomalous" readings and left it at that, until someone on the High-Rig doing routine checks spotted something in the same geostationary orbit.

The fact that *something* was in that orbit nearly caused a minor world war. The United Northern States and Provinces accused the Muslim-Catholic Alliance. MusCat blamed the Pan-Asian Confederation. The PAC claimed IT as theirs, but stated that they'd launched it only in retaliation against Old Europe who had criticized their human rights record (not to mention industrial profligacy). Old Europe, as usual, blamed everyone else merely for existing. And so it went around.

I suppose I should introduce myself. I'm Antoine Solomon Murphy, a space engineer with a specialism in self-organizing orbital construction--SpaceHabs. I've been known universally as just "Murphy" (or sometimes "Murph" with close friends) since about the age of seven. Unfortunately that also carries its own burden--"Murphy's Law."

If it can go wrong, it will. How many times have I heard

that? How many times were random events summarily tagged as my fault? Later I decided to replace this with a new rule: "Adequate preparation and intelligence can cope with any situation."

I work for the Independent Space Habitat Research Agency, ISHRA. (You've probably seen the "Build. Life." ad series.) As we're the closest thing to an orbital troubleshooting team, we were the ones called in to figure IT out.

IT's orbit was perfect. That ruled out the MusCat Alliance immediately--those yoyos couldn't plan a trajectory if their lives (or Yahweh's) depended on it. *Too* perfect; even the Pan-Asians and Old Europe would struggle to launch something that precisely.

It had to be alien and that was worrying in several ways. First, was IT benign? (I'm talking about political-nonthink now — let's face it, have you ever met a politician who understood logic?) Was IT crewed? If so, could we (and should we) try to help? If we tried would they understand? And the biggie: how could we establish contact?

I was given twelve hours to put together my team. We'd be the lucky ones who'd get a close look at IT. I took the whole twelve hours. Not to choose my team — I knew that in less than a minute — but I wanted time to think about the approach. I've also found that the "higher-ups" get nervous when you give them an answer "too quickly."

I gave my boss the list and a request for a launch window for Mickey Mouse, ISHRA's space hopper — so called because of the twin Doppler radar/LASER range finders on each side of the vessel that look like large ears.

"Good team, Murphy." Pasierowski barely scanned the names.

To say I was surprised would be an understatement. I'd been ready for at least an hour of wrangling over each one. The fact they'd all find it incredibly cool wasn't much of a bargaining point — ISHRA doesn't have the most progressive management style.

"The MKY011 Hopper is not an option though."

No-one outside senior management uses Mickey Mouse's official designation — the second reason for its peppy nickname. Without the Hopper we'd be limited to remote investigation, which would provide a fraction of the information we'd get from a crewed mission. "Listen, Boss." I smiled at Pasierowski's slight grimace; he hates being called that. "We aren't going to figure this thing out sitting a couple of thousand kilometers away."

"The Hopper isn't big enough."

"Huh?" I figured he'd finally gone nuts, then I realized he was still avoiding eye contact and the OmniBuck dropped. "Who is it?"

Pasierowski traced random patterns on his desk. "You'll be joined by Lieutenant Devuyst."

"The military? What's their interest in this?"

"You're not *that* naive, Murphy. This comes from the First Minister herself. The military are providing the vehicle and the pilot."

"What about our remote sensors?"

"They have everything for close proximity operations."

My responses were limited and I used the shortest one for efficiency. Cat — Caitlin — was always our main pilot and would *not* be happy. *If it can go wrong...* I cursed inwardly for even starting the thought. I should have anticipated military interest and prepared for it.

"You'll be picked up at zero six hundred hours." Pasierowski shrugged. "It's still the chance of a lifetime."

The trip to the High-Rig was the usual combination of tedium mixed with equal parts nausea and excitement. Climbing up a tether to orbit isn't the quickest way of getting there, but it's attractively cheap to management. This time there was also resentment when I mentioned the military. Even Chun, the least outspoken person I've ever met, had only bad things to say. "Soldiers attach guns to everything. Aliens not very happy."

When we reached the military hopper his judgment was confirmed. The front of the snub craft was littered by several large guns and heavy beam projectors, plus several other nasty looking devices whose purpose I could only guess at. Devuyst was waiting, standing at ease with her hands behind her back.

"We're prepped for immediate launch. If you'll take your positions we can get going." Devuyst spoke with the kind of clipped tones that came from dealing with subordinates who responded without question.

"Don't we need orientation first?" Cat's voice was low and thick. "You know, basics like safety, command transfer procedures..."

Devuyst shook her head. "Negative, Ms. Storey. This operation is strictly military and we operate on a need-to-know basis."

Cat tipped her head to one side. "Then you don't need us and we shouldn't even be here. Murphy? What is this? Since *when* are basic safety and operating protocols a 'secret'?"

Cat was right; no one went on a ship — even just a Hopper — without familiarizing themselves with the capabilities and orienting a secondary pilot. In fact the law required it. "Lieutenant..." I examined the space between my feet for several seconds. "According to Scharpman-Raynes we can't even enter that ship without either Operator's Certification or conducting a full orientation session. I'm sure you understand the importance of due diligence in safety matters."

"The Scharpman-Raynes Act doesn't apply, Dr. Murphy. This is a military operation, not covered by civil restrictions." Her voice was controlled, but her teeth were clenched. Evidently this scenario hadn't been considered.

"That's true, but we're civilians. I'd be much happier if we had someone to back you up. Just in case."

"Murph!" Cat started to speak, but much to my relief didn't continue.

"That's not part of my orders." Devuyst's jaw seemed to jut out.

"A lot of people went to great lengths to bring us together, Lieutenant. I wouldn't want to tell them we failed at the first hurdle, would you?" I waited and eventually she shook her head almost imperceptibly. "I understand you weren't ordered to brief a co-pilot, but were you ordered *not* to?"

I hoped Devuyst wasn't locked into the narrow constraints of the typical military mindset. I really didn't want to have to step in between her and Cat.

"I received no orders on the matter."

"In that case, I'd appreciate it if you'd explain the controls to Ms. Storey." I smiled my most friendly smile. "Naturally you don't need to include details of weapons or other sensitive systems."

"I wouldn't."

Devuyst spun on her heel, grabbed the handholds and slithered through the 'Lock feet first. I heard someone blow a raspberry behind me but didn't bother to check who. I just hoped Devuyst hadn't caught it.

The Hopper was larger than Mickey Mouse and I wondered just how maneuverable it would be in orbit, especially if we had to carry out close proximity operations. Inside the flat black hull — another difference, most orbital craft are white and highly reflective to ward off radiation — it was even more cramped than inside Mickey Mouse. Passengers with swinging cats need not apply.

I twisted into the seat next to Devuyst, leaving enough DNA samples along the way to convict me in a murder case. "You military types must enjoy each other's company." I tried another smile but it splintered against the Lieutenant's cold glare as she continued her pre-flight checks.

"It's armored, Murph." Cat thumped the hull as she slid into the co-pilot's seat behind Devuyst, managing to somehow still look elegant as she did. The hull didn't ring like normal; instead there was a dull "thunk". "Dumb military think we're going to be fighting off space aliens."

I saw Devuyst's shoulders tighten but her voice was as emotionless as ever. "Would you rather be defenseless and unprotected?"

Chun spoke for the first time since meeting Devuyst, his slick raven hair reflecting reds and purples from the operating lights. "Your reasoning is weak. IT must have traveled dozens of light-years at the least. Whoever sent it control energies far beyond anything we're capable of. PlaSteel armor and guns will prove only that we're belligerent, unintelligent, and a *very* minor threat."

Devuyst pinned me in my seat with a withering glance. "You didn't tell them we're not the only ones interested in IT?"

"Murphy? What happened?" Cat sounded hurt.

I sighed. "Eighteen hours ago Pan-Asia directed one of their MilSats to intercept IT and establish 'communications'."

"Communications?" Chun's interest peaked now we were talking about his specialty. "What kind? Digital? Analogue? Radio? Light?"

Chun is a communications savant. He can build a high fidelity communication system using anything from a laser to a length of dog intestine and some paper cups. He's also a linguistics expert fluent in fifteen languages and studies dead languages for fun. In-between he bolsters his tan while surfing and listening to mid-twentieth rock and roll. Chun says the music helps him think better. A scary thought, as he's already in the top one percent.

"The signals showed the deployment of a point five megawatt coherent optical broadcast." I knew they weren't going to buy that, but my hands were somewhat tied.

I wasn't surprised when Chun got there first. "They tried to shoot it down?"

"Officially they tried to establish 'contact' and there was a malfunction."

"Malfunction my a-"

"Cat. They tried and failed. That's all we need to know."

"What about the MilSat?" Chun asked the big question.

I shrugged. "Lieutenant?"

Devuyst didn't turn from the controls. "The MilSat was lost."

"IT destroyed the Sat? Are you serious?" said Cat.

"The MilSat deployed and twenty milliseconds later stopped. No signals were subsequently detected. The Pan-Asians withdrew and our remote scans show IT and nothing else."

"Have the Pan-Asians said anything?"

"Communications malfunction."

Silence descended on the cramped flight deck like heat before a thunder-storm. Everyone had their own thoughts, but no one was sharing.

Devuyst grinned for the first time. "Retracting umbilicals. Disengaging docking clamps. Firing thrusters two, four and six. Five second burst at eighty percent capacity. On my Mark. We'll clear the station and I'll familiarize Ms. Storey with the controls. Unless anyone wants to leave now?" She paused briefly. "Much as I enjoy your chatter, I find I prefer the quiet. And Mark!"

It didn't take long to familiarize Cat with the military hopper. She'd raced rocket planes in university and could easily have picked up a big juicy pro contract when she finished her studies. Luckily for us she decided to pursue her academic interests instead. Thirty minutes later Devuyst reluctantly admitted that Cat could pilot the ship competently.

Devuyst took us high out of Earth's orbit in a long and dreary maneuver that I was pleased to say I mostly slept through. Then she dropped planet-ward once again in a trajectory that seemed odd to me, but one Cat interpreted immediately.

"You want to come at IT out of the Sun? Murph — she's trying to sneak up on it like we're playing tag."

"I'm sure IT will know we're here whichever way you go, Lieutenant," I said.

"That isn't the only reason." Devuyst growled. "We'll have the best view on approach."

Cat gave a snort. "Sure, *that's* the reason."

"It also aligns us for a coded-neutrino burst."

"Coded neutrinos? From where?" I was starting to share Cat's unease. "Are we going to make the same mistake the Pan-Asians did?"

"The source is classified. We believe the level is low enough not to be threatening." Devuyst kept her hands on the controls.

"But you don't know for sure." Cat said.

"It's a calculated risk." She glanced back. "Either way, we're approaching alignment and will know in twenty-five seconds."

"*We're* the ones taking the risk though." Cat shook her head. "What happens if that thing decides to make us disappear too?"

"Target in visual range." Devuyst maximized the optical feed and a long, roughly cylindrical-looking blob appeared.

"Enhancing."

The image rippled as the computer ran optimizing algorithms, making a guess as to IT's appearance. After a few minutes the image steadied into something resembling a cross between a skyscraper and a trash can.

"That's IT?" Chun asked. "Are you serious?"

"A garbage can in space?" The corners of my mouth twitched.

Chun laughed and a second later we were all at it. Except Devuyst.

"The optimization program is finding it hard to lock down the appearance. What you're seeing is an approximation."

"I could do better. This is stupid." Cat tried to hold back her giggles but failed. "Maybe IT's really a giant mop and broom?"

"Switching to raw visuals." Devuyst's fingers flicked over the keys and the image changed back to the blurry shape. "Holding at ten thousand meters. Deploying neutrino detectors."

Several faint metallic vibrations resonated through the small cabin and I assumed that some of the anonymous devices we'd seen on the front of the craft had detached. Now *I* was starting to get uptight. Neutrino detectors are huge; most are several kilometers across and buried underground. "How are you going to catch these neutrinos? With a baseball mitt?"

"The neutrinos themselves are spin-encoded by the emitter. By aligning the emitter and detector appropriately we can get a shadow scan of the inside of the target. I'll feed the images onto your screens."

My screen lit up with a murky gray image of swirling white noise, like a video taken inside a sandstorm with a monochrome camera. At the bottom a frame counter ticked off the milliseconds. A sliver of black appeared, growing and stretching. It might have been a systems diagnostic or the calling card of the long lost Mars Colony for all I knew. Then it shrank back down to nothing and vanished.

Cat guffawed. "You got nothing! All that drama and mystery and you didn't get a single sliver of information."

"What do you mean?" I asked.

"Do a 3D projection on the scans." Cat said.

Devuyst manipulated the controls with tight fingers. The image snapped up on my screen in three dimensions: a perfect black rendering with the same outline as IT.

"The neutrinos didn't penetrate?" I said.

"I thought... that is... I mean that's not supposed to be possible is it?" Devuyst frowned.

"At our level of technology it's not. If you had enough energy you might be able to generate a field strong enough to deflect them."

"We'd detect a field that strong." Devuyst sounded confident and I wondered why. No doubt she wouldn't be "at liberty" to share the knowledge.

"We don't know how that might work. How would we know what to detect, or even recognize it if we did?" Cat said.

Cat was right, but we still had a job to do. "We'll have

to do this the old fashioned way. Can you take us closer, Lieutenant?"

Devuyst's knuckles whitened as she gripped the edge of the console. "That's my call, Dr. Murphy. This is still a military mission. This is a minor setback. You know what they say, if it can go wr-"

I held up my hand. "Please. I'd rather you didn't."

"What? Oh yes, I see."

I smiled appreciatively. At least I hoped she realized it was a smile and not me just baring my teeth at her. "If you have a better suggestion, please go ahead."

I saw Devuyst's larynx moving and realized she was sub-vocalizing. No doubt querying the military "brains" via a communications implant. Several minutes passed before she spoke.

"We're going in. But we back off at the first sign of trouble. And I define trouble, no one else."

"Can I make a suggestion?" Cat said.

Devuyst didn't look up from the controls.

"We have remote probes. We could send them ahead to get a better idea of what IT is. I can fly one and Murphy here might remember the basics."

"Thanks Cat. Your confidence is underwhelming." I thought about making a rude gesture, but decided against it.

"That makes sense." Devuyst said. "I'll transfer control to your stations."

The Hopper vibrated as the probes launched and data immediately appeared on my screen.

Cat gave me a big thumbs up. "Telemetry reading Five-By,"

"Okay. I'll try the rear and see what kind of propulsion this thing has. Assuming it has a propulsion system and it's at the rear." I worked the controls steadily.

"You also assume it has a rear." Chun laughed.

"I'll take a sweep length-wise and take a look at the 'front'." Cat worked the controls. "The probe has a lot of juice."

It was true, as I found out when I laid in my own instructions — easily twice as fast as the probes on Mickey Mouse. The military is never starved of expensive equipment. Not that I would want to swap with them. All the equipment going can't compensate for having to figuratively check in your brain when you sign up.

IT's image grew steadily as the probe boosted forwards, rapidly leaving us behind. The display danced occasionally as the sensors rescaled, keeping IT squarely in frame. Dragging my fingers over the control surface I zoomed the image onto the area we assumed to be the rear. The cylindrical shape increased in radius at this point, split by a number of channels running back from a ring of mountainous blocks girdling the waist.

The surface was like nothing I'd seen. It didn't look metallic despite what the earlier reports said; it also didn't look like one of the lattice structures we were trying to grow as space habitats. I'd secretly hoped (irrationally) that IT would validate our approach and help end the ever-present funding squeeze. IT's surface seemed more knitted or woven, but even as I watched I realized its appearance was shifting constantly.

"Some kind of field effect?" Cat had spotted it too. "A residual from the jump to our Solar System?"

"Jump?" Devuyst hovered over the controls.

"If IT came through normal space we'd have picked it up a long time before it was in orbit."

I twisted the probe on the Y axis to get a passing view. It wasn't as big as Clarke's "Rama", but big enough to be impressive: at least four hundred meters across by my estimate. The outer shell opened up into a matrix of heavy supports that wove around what appeared to be some form of ducting.

An opening slid onto the screen, a hole with deep, perfectly shadowed walls exposing IT's interior. "My god..."

The whisper was mine but I heard everyone gasp. Inside was something that looked like a captured star in the inverse — a huge black sphere that crackled as vari-colored plasma waves washed across its surface. "Is that what I think it is?" I asked, not really expecting an answer.

"If that's a black-hole, something is shielding us from its gravitational effects," Cat mused. "At this distance we, the Earth and Moon, plus anything in orbit would be sucked in."

Other than the possible black-hole there wasn't much else to see. Rather there was an overwhelming amount to see, but without any kind of reference it was hard to know what was worthy of attention. We could spend hours studying the alien equivalent of a rivet and pass over a warp drive without noticing.

Cat's probe skimmed just above the surface of IT. The surface tapered slightly, forming a flattened end dominated by an inset crenelated ring.

"Airlock?" Chun asked.

"Maybe." Cat checked something. "If it is, it's over fifty meters across."

"It could be a porthole for a very large weapon," said Devuyst.

"Can we drop the paranoia?" I sighed. "Any suggestions?"

"Perhaps we should try communicating with it. We know violence is unlikely to achieve anything." Cat smiled innocently. "Other than testosterone-inspired suicide."

Devuyst snapped around to face Cat, then took a breath and shrugged. "If you think it will do any good."

"Now we're talking!" Chun said. "What comms facilities do we have?"

"We can transmit and receive on all known EM spectrum: radio, light, laser. We also have sealed, encrypted quantum channels and audio."

"Maybe we should try the last one," Cat said. "If the Lieutenant shouts loud enough, maybe she can intimidate IT into communicating."

"We should keep it simple." Chun was lost in his own world. "I'd suggest we try light initially — it's probably the most natural communication medium for any kind of intelligent life.

It should also be seen as harmless — as long as we don't try something like the Pan-Asians."

It made sense. The Universe is filled with light and it was the night stars that first inspired an early human race with collective dreams. Although that could be an anthropomorphic viewpoint rather than a universal constant. "What frequency?"

Chun's fingers stopped drumming momentarily. "We'd have to scan."

Devuyst turned to the controls. "I can set up a program to fire patterns at random frequencies to-"

"The military answer — spray and pray. Let me..." Chun caressed his controls, cutting through the various options like he'd been using the system for years. "I'll set up simple repeated pulses at regular intervals. Twenty should be enough. Then we can start in the middle frequency and shift either way using binary partitioning-"

"What the hell ?" Devuyst turned to me. "He's accessing primary systems interfaces from his console, bypassing security interlocks, running through classified... you're not supposed to be able to do that."

"Chun, slow down. You need to explain-"

An oily metallic click caught everyone's attention. Devuyst had produced a heavy looking pistol from bog-knew-where and it was pointing directly at Chun's face. "Hands off the controls."

"What the hell? Murphy?" Chun's hands trembled as he lifted them. "I'm doing my job."

"Put the gun down. Are you going to risk depressurizing the whole ship you dumb grunt?" Cat spoke quietly, but her tone told me she was about to do something we'd probably all regret. Why I'd been put in charge of a team like this, I really had to wonder.

"Yeah, put it down, jeez... I mean please."

Chun was looking for my support, but strictly speaking I was helpless. Devuyst was right, this was a military mission. We were simply guests who might just happen to be useful at some point. Nevertheless, the situation needed some calm.

"Lieutenant." I spoke with deliberate softness. "We understand you're in charge here. We're trying to help. We're not used to working under military guidelines, so forgive our ignorance. Chun is a communications expert and, although he got a little too enthusiastic, he certainly didn't mean any harm."

Devuyst didn't waver. "If he makes another unauthorized move I *will* shoot him. Or anyone else who tries to sabotage this mission."

My pulse thumped in my temple. "You don't really want to shoot anyone, Lieutenant."

"Don't count on that."

"You'd have to shoot all of us, which I don't think is practical." I reached out slowly, trying to stop my hand from shaking. "I think it would be better if you give me the gun."

I heard murmurs of agreement and counted seventeen heavy thumps in my head before Devuyst engaged the safety, and reholstered it rather than giving it to me. The collected sighs seemed to lower the air pressure in the cabin several points and I decided not to press the point. "Unless there are any better suggestions, I think we should get closer and let Chun get to work."

I hoped nobody spotted the trickle of sweat I felt running down the back of my neck.

Chun turned back to his console and started working the controls very deliberately. "I'm setting up a sequence and programming the sensors to 'listen'. The synchronized readings should be able to match any response to a specific frequency range. These systems aren't designed to work like this, so it will take a while."

After several minutes Chun triggered the sequence and we watched the graphs. At 730 Nanometers, Chun laughed softly. "Definite response detected. An energy build-up. I'd say we got IT's attention."

"Dangerous?" I was thinking of the Pan-Asian Sat.

Devuyst answered. "No. Very low level. Possibly a sub-system activating."

Chun nodded. "I'll start with a sequence of rising even-numbers followed by primes and then odd-numbers. Hopefully that will establish our signals as both artificial and somewhat intelligent."

"Hopefully?" Devuyst glanced at Chun. "Aren't you the expert?"

"I am." Chun smiled, displaying not even the slightest hint of modesty. "But even-numbers followed by primes and odd-numbers might be the biggest insult in IT's vocabulary for all I know."

Devuyst unlocked the thrusters and another set of controls that I could only speculate on. My guess made me uncomfortable so I kept it to myself.

Chun triggered the signal and IT's hull brightened as the coded sequences bounced erratically off the ever-changing surface. The broadcast lasted less than a minute before the inside of the Hopper lit up. Every external feed had maxed out and overloaded the screens. Bright enough that Chun could have worked on his tan if he had time. "IT repeated our signal back to us, vastly speeded up and on all frequencies." Chun hesitated. "There's something else..."

My screen dimmed slowly as the system re-adjusted and, edge by edge, IT came back into view.

"Does everyone see that?" Cat sounded almost reverential.

The "airlock" was opening steadily, individual pie-slice segments simply vanishing as we watched. When the last one was gone a pure white light flared up, surrounding the inner surface of what was now a definite hole. I saw Devuyst flick her thumbs to the fire-controls then relax. I was thankful that her judgment was as quick as her reflexes.

"Let's go in." Cat was always the eager explorer.

"They might think that's an unfriendly act." Devuyst glanced sideways at me. "Don't you think?"

I was flattered that she asked. "I'd say *that* is an invitation."

"You don't know that." Devuyst said. "And you don't know

what's in there."

I shrugged. "We never will, sitting here."

"If we send a probe closer, we may be able to see something inside." Chun suggested.

Cat worked her controls, bringing her probe down and closer to IT, correcting smoothly with the thrusters until the camera pointed directly through the hole.

"What's that?" Devuyst hissed through clenched teeth.

It was hard to make out clearly. A shimmering layer filled the opening, an impossible liquid pool that distorted and warped the view inside.

"An atmospheric meniscus?" I wondered out loud. "It's something we've discussed as a theoretical possibility."

"What holds it in?" Devuyst glanced at me. "A force field?"

"Beats me." I turned to Chun. "Can you compensate for the distortion?"

Chun frowned. "Sorry, Murph. We don't have enough 'horsepower' on board. Maybe back at the office, but that'll take time."

Everyone was silent. Finally Cat spoke with a distinct challenge in her voice. "Well, we can sit here and contemplate IT, or take action."

"I agree." Devuyst spoke up. "The situation's unpredictable and potentially dangerous. We should destroy IT."

I groaned. When would the military mind realize "kill 'em all" isn't a one-size-fits-all solution.

"How would we do that? Do we have anything that could cause even the slightest scratch to IT?" My patience was running out.

Devuyst didn't respond. Her chin seemed to get more pronounced as she pretended to inspect the uninteresting display before her.

"We could send the probe in," Chun suggested.

It was a good idea and might give us information about what was inside. Assuming IT would allow us to send a probe in. It was also a long shot that we'd be able to stay in touch with it if we did, but had to be worth trying.

"Those probes cost the government over a million each. Only a civilian would think of throwing that away," Devuyst snapped.

"We're using it for scientific research not throwing it away." Cat smiled at Devuyst. "Secondly, governments don't have any money —they have the taxpayers' money. I'm sure people would rather their taxes were used to research an alien craft than to kill more people."

"Not everyone shares your pacifist views, Ms. Storey."

"Enough." I had to raise my voice, even in the confines of the Hopper. "It's either the probe or us. Your call, Lieutenant."

I caught Devuyst sub-vocalizing on her secret channel again and smiled. This time she even had the decency to redden slightly. "That strategy is acceptable."

The probe edged forwards, approaching the shimmering layer at a leisurely two meters per second, hardly fast enough to muss your hair. I manipulated the second probe so it tracked its twin, zooming in to capture as much detail as possible.

"We're still sending everything to ISHRA aren't we, Chun? I'd sure hate for them to miss this."

"All *permitted* data feeds are in the green." He sniffed. "Presumably all the secret ones are operating as expected."

"Contact in thirty seconds," Cat announced, "And five, four, three, two, one-"

The front manipulator arm contacted the surface and the probe vanished.

"What the hell?" Devuyst scanned the controls, her larynx working at a feverish pace. "What just happened?"

"Cat? Chun? Anyone catch it?"

"We've lost the probe." Cat's voice was calm and I wondered how mine sounded. "Time sync to the point of contact. Then nothing. No telemetry, remote pickups all show dead, feedback CPR non-existent, no IR or radar signature. It just vanished."

"Destroyed?" Devuyst asked.

"Unknown." Cat answered.

"Inside?" I tried to sound positive.

"Unknown."

I hoped the recording from the second probe would show us what happened and replayed the optical feed in slow motion. The close-up showed the manipulator arm brush the "meniscus" and the probe disappeared.

"It went inside," Cat announced.

Devuyst groaned. "You're making that up."

"I saw motion too." Chun said quietly.

I hated to admit it but Devuyst seemed right. I hadn't seen anything to suggest the probe hadn't disintegrated and said so. Cat didn't agree.

"If it had been destroyed we'd have picked up a heat signature or something. Play it again, Murph. Slowest rate."

I restarted the video and watched the probe move forward. It was so painfully slow, you could almost imagine seeing individual atoms if you could zoom in far enough. The arm touched the surface. The probe blurred, and by the next frame it had vanished. "That was definitely motion blur."

"I saw it disintegrate in a dust cloud." Devuyst stared straight ahead.

"That's... Murphy, do we really need to listen to this? The meniscus changed as it went through. That thing is an airlock, not a weapon."

Cat was frustrated and I sympathized. How much evidence of non-belligerence would it take to convince Devuyst? "The three scientists on this mission agree that the probe entered IT. Whatever blocked the neutrino scan is also stopping us receiving any probe data. Just a suggestion, but you might want to communicate that to your bosses. I'm sure they'd agree the next logical step is for us to follow the probe."

Devuyst hesitated only momentarily before sending her report. I could only wonder what spin she put on it.

"They'll contact us once a decision is made."

The Hopper slipped into a silence that extended into

long minutes until I would have given a week's pay just to hear someone cough.

Cat obliged. "Why are you here, Lieutenant?"

"What do you mean?" Devuyst's voice was low as she looked at each of us in turn.

"Murph here is a genius in space construction, or so he likes to tell his all-too-rare dates. Chun is a linguistics, communications and technology expert. I'm a licensed space pilot and qualified chemical engineer. What qualifies you?"

Cat was trying to goad Devuyst and I should have spoken up, but I was interested in the answer too.

"I have nearly ten years' combat experience. I'm a fully trained deep-space navigator.' She smiled towards Cat. "Not just a Terra-Luna pilot. I've served in every major campaign since signing up and also three deep-space missions."

"That's quite a record, Lieutenant." I hoped to forestall Cat, but it didn't work.

"Murph's right. But there must be many others with similar records. Why you and not them?"

"Well," Devuyst paused. "I was part of the team that pulled off the only one-hundred percent casualty-free space rescue. *Someone* thought you people were important enough to get me."

Chun grinned broadly. "You saved Elvis VII!"

A hundred or so years back the sightings were just a legend. Who would have suspected the little genetic secret hidden in the bowels of Graceland? Elvis VII was the first truly successful clone. Despite the highly publicized kidnapping and rescue, he had little musical talent and eventually chose to exile himself.

"What was he like? Did you speak with him? Did he really sing all the way down from orbit?" Chun looked like a ten year old who'd just been given a double allowance.

"Well, he was like... Elvis." Devuyst shrugged. "He mumbled a lot and did that hip thing too much."

"Man he had it all: fame, fortune, a great tan, Paris IV.

Why would he give that up to become a MusCat Minister?"

"He had everything — except talent." Cat chuckled.

"Come on Cat, that's no way to-"

I was about to wade in to defuse the situation. Chun was the perfect logician in everything, except rock and roll, but a proximity warning filled the Hopper.

"What?" I checked the screens. "Anyone see it?"

Devuyst gasped. "It's the probe."

I flipped viewpoint and sure enough there was the probe floating just outside the meniscus, looking like nothing had happened.

"Telemetry resumed. Five by." Cat said. "Ninety-three minutes and ten seconds since blackout."

"Diagnostics are green." Chun announced. "As though it never left."

"Data logs?"

Devuyst worked her controls and shook her head. "The logs are there, but nothing was collected while it was inside."

"Now what?"

"Hold." Devuyst said, sending another private communication. Several minutes passed. "They want us to send the probe in again."

Cat took control and guided the probe back to the airlock and it vanished. Ninety-three minutes later it reappeared unharmed. Two further attempts had the same results. The last time we sent in both probes and they both returned intact.

After the last attempt Devuyst held up her hand. "Message from Central." She listened intently. "We're cleared to attempt entry."

"Thank goodness they saw sense." Cat manipulated her controls. "I'll set the second probe to record our entrance."

"If you want to record a message for someone," said Deyvust, "This might be your last chance."

I don't think any of us had thought about that before and the walls seemed to tighten around us. Unless we could find a way to communicate with the controllers of IT, this really could be a one way trip. "If it doesn't toss us out after ninety-three minutes, will we be able to communicate with our people from the inside?" I wasn't hopeful.

"If neutrinos can't penetrate, nothing we have will. Getting cold feet? I thought you were certain the aliens would be friendly."

"I am..." Suddenly I wasn't quite so sure.

"Then there's no reason they'd hold us." Devuyst activated the controls. "Thrusters in thirty seconds."

The push from the thrusters pressed me back in my seat and we drifted closer. Our velocity seemed to drop as we approached. The instruments showed our speed as constant; any apparent change was purely psychological.

The silver field filled the Hopper with dancing light. It would have been nauseating if my stomach wasn't already knotted tight. The front of the ship brushed the glittering surface and my insides were dragged in a direction I'd never felt before. My vision blurred with intense smears of blinding light, visible even with my eyes clenched.

There was a slight clunk and as soon as I could see fully, I checked the external views. All they showed though was a milky whiteness.

"There's some flash frosting." Devuyst checked her controls. "It should clear in a couple of minutes. Sensors are picking up heat and atmosphere out there."

"What kind of atmosphere?" I asked.

"The sensors are fluctuating. Or the atmosphere is. Mostly hydrogen, some carbon dioxide. Wait a sec-"

"I saw it too," said Cat. "A sudden spike of oxygen that wasn't there before. Nitrogen levels increasing too. Murph, it's replicating our atmosphere."

"How does IT know about our atmosphere?" Devuyst was immediately suspicious. "They haven't scanned us yet."

"How would you know if they had?" Chun was enjoying Devuyst's discomfort.

"External atmosphere and temperature now match ours within instrumentation limits," Cat announced. "I think we're being invited outside."

Chun tapped his control panel. "The pickups are clearing too."

I flipped through the optical feeds. We were in a chamber around three hundred meters long and perhaps a little under half that wide. At the far end a large flickering surface covered with strange patterns dominated the wall. It could have been a display screen, or — for all I knew — a meaningless piece of decoration. The walls were punctuated by a number of semitransparent enclosures full of shadows that hinted at their contents.

"Are those...?" Devuyst tailed off.

"Lifeforms?" I zoomed in on the shadows in a useless attempt to make out more detail. How do you make sense of something that you can only partially see and have never seen before? "Maybe."

"Crew? A sleeper ship?" Cat asked.

"The crew are asleep?" Devuyst manipulated her own controls. "I can't get a good view."

"Infrared shows nothing, just ambient temperature." Cat said. "If they're alive, metabolizing that is, they're either shielded or doing so at levels below those we can detect."

"Suspended animation." Chun didn't look up. "Necessary for traveling astronomical distances."

"That would only be needed if this ship traveled at sublight speeds though," Cat said. "Which it didn't. Otherwise we would have detected it before it-"

"You don't know that," Chun broke in. "How much faster than light can they travel? How far have they come?"

"Reasonable assumptions, based on what we know. If they can travel FTL, it should be effectively instantaneous-"

"Reasonable to us, maybe not for them. We can't make that kind of assumption. If space-time exists for them at all, we need to consider the possibility that-"

"Now who's making assumptions?"

The logic-chopping was fascinating, but I had more pressing concerns. "Can we leave this till later? Has anyone checked communications? Are we on our own?"

Devuyst ran through the comms channels, no doubt checking her super-secret lines as well as the regular channels. "Everything is blocked as we thought."

"In that case, we might as well have a look." Three serious faces turned towards me. "We're not going to achieve anything shut in here and we have less than seventy-five minutes left until we leave."

Devuyst nodded and popped the main hatch. A rush of air washed over us, but something wasn't quite right. It's amazing how you adapt to your environment. You can completely block out the combined body odor of four people shut inside a small Hopper for hours, but as soon as the hatch opens you realize what you've been living in. Here the air outside smelled the same as inside. IT had replicated the Hopper's atmosphere down to the very last detail, something that scared me.

Chun was the first to unfasten his restraints. He lifted himself cautiously, a reaction common to anyone who's worked in varying gravity fields, then hopped to his feet. "We have gravity." He bounced up and down. "Feels like one-gee."

"IT simulated everything else, why not gravity too?" Cat unbuckled herself and slid through the hatch.

"We carry our atmosphere with us — how would IT know our gravity?" Devuyst asked.

"Maybe they scanned Earth and made an assumption? Maybe they can tell from adaptations in our skeletal structure? Who knows?"

"Nobody here but us soy-chickens." Cat winked at me as I clambered through the narrow hatch with Devuyst bringing up the rear.

"Unless you count them." I gestured at the enclosures on the wall.

"Possibly..." said Cat. "I'm going to take a look."

Chun nodded toward the end of the chamber. "I want to check that out and-"

"Wait a second." I held up my hands. "We shouldn't wander around alone. Right, Lieutenant?"

"Stay in pairs. Full environmental gear. This atmosphere could disappear as fast as it came."

"Right." I pointed at Cat and she grabbed her helmet from the floor. "How about you and the Lieutenant investigate the 'things', while me and Chun take a look at the 'screen'?"

Devuyst stiffened. "I'd be more productive working with Chun."

Cat shrugged, but said nothing.

"Okay. Let's do that." I rushed to catch up with Cat.

"She's insufferable, Murph."

"I've worked with better people." I kept my voice low as well. "It's only one mission though. After this we can go back to building SpaceHabs. Do you think those really are lifeforms?"

"If it annoys the military bitch, I do." She giggled a little too loudly. "Cat by name, cat by nature. Come on, let's take a look."

The shapes were no clearer as we approached; in fact they seemed less distinct. At arm's length they were just a mass of dark and light blotches behind clear panels and did nothing to ease my concerns.

"Those are only a few centimeters deep aren't they?" Cat reached out and ran her hand over the clear material. "Not hot or cold. Just a covering..."

"Covering nothing?" The whole thing gave me the creeps.

"Exactly. Like a movie set that makes you think there's something there but isn't."

"Could it be artistic or decorative?"

"Sure, but how would we know?"

I heard a metallic sound from the other side of the Hopper.

"Hey... don't!" Chun said.

"I'm not going to hurt it. Don't worry."

We rushed round the ship and saw Devuyst working a

pry-bar at a small panel near the bottom of the "screen." It seemed futile and I was about to say so when a blue-white flash engulfed her. She was silhouetted momentarily as her scream filled the chamber.

I'll give her credit; Cat didn't hesitate and ran forward to pull Devuyst away from the panel. She rolled her on to her back and checked her vitals.

"Oh jeez... that hurts... do something, please." Devuyst moaned, thrashing on the floor as Cat tried to hold her still.

I reached out and turned her hands over. Her environment suit gloves were charred all the way through and when I probed deeper it was clear her hands had suffered a similar fate. "Chun, get the medical pack. Cat, we're going to have to get these gloves off."

She nodded and held Devuyst tighter.

"Wha ya... doing?" Devuyst responded to the pressure, but didn't really seem very aware.

"Shush. We're taking care of you."

I unlocked the wrist seals, pinched the tattered remnants and with a quick jerk pulled both gloves off. Devuyst screamed, twisting in Cat's arms but didn't break free.

Chun dropped to his knees, already tearing open the medical pack, and placed a Dexofentanil inhaler cup over Devuyst's nose and mouth. Rummaging through the rest of the supplies with his spare hand he tossed me a pair of sterile gloves and a tube of burns cream.

Devuyst grew still, her breath turning shallow and a little ragged. I rubbed half the tube over her fingers, then squirted the remainder into the gloves before slipping them onto her discolored hands.

"How long does that last?" I indicated the inhaler.

Chun checked. "It says seven to nine hours."

"That's plenty. Okay, let's get her in the ship and the rest of us. We don't have long."

We made Devuyst as comfortable as we could in one of the Hopper seats and I took the pistol from her belt. The last thing we needed was her armed in a drug-induced haze. Then we waited, the uncomfortable silence seeming to stretch for hours. Eventually I checked the time; we were a long way past the ninety-three minute mark.

I swore quietly and scrambled out of the Hopper, followed by Chun and Cat. "Looks like we're not going home yet. What happened, Chun?"

Chun explained that they'd decided that the wall area might provide a communication function. Devuyst had spotted the panel and decided it must conceal an interface. Chun warned her it was unlikely, but she'd gone ahead and tried to get the cover off anyway.

"Did you get anything?" I asked.

"I've not really started. It's not like any technology I've seen — no surprise there — but my gut tells me it's some kind of comms system. Those patterns, they're not just random."

"Language?" asked Cat.

"I have to work on that assumption. Translation, which may not be possible, would take years. With no common reference points it would be harder to decipher than Etruscan — at least they were human."

"Not a good bet. Could we fly out?"

"I doubt it, Murph." Cat chewed her lip. "The Hopper hasn't got the boost to overcome one-gee. Do we even know how we got in?"

"Climb out?" Chun gestured at the airlock.

It was at least ten meters up and I didn't see much in the way of hand or footholds. "That looks impossible in an environmental suit and even if we made it, then what?"

"Four hours in the suits maybe. Someone might pick up our signals in time..." Cat didn't sound optimistic.

"And the Lieutenant?"

Cat breathed out slowly. "She'd need gloves..."

"There!" Chun jumped closer to the screen. "I've definitely seen that pattern before. It has to be language."

"If IT wanted to communicate, wouldn't it just use a language we'd understand?" I waved my hands. "It adapted to our environmental needs, couldn't it just pluck Standard English from our minds?"

"Language is a lot harder than biochemistry." Chun studied the patterns intensely. "Who knows what IT can do though. Maybe it just needs more data..."

"You mean language?" Cat frowned. "What are you going to do? Talk to IT?"

"Sure, why not? What do you think, Murph? Worth a shot?"

I had to admit I was bewildered by the idea too, but our options were limited.

"Okay. You talk to the wall. Cat, take a closer look at the airlock. Maybe it has a reverse. But make sure you don't trip it! I'll check on the Lieutenant."

Devuyst opened her eyes as I approached.

"How do you feel?"

"Numb. No pain. Am I going to be okay?" Her mouth trembled. "This was supposed to be my last assignment. I'd applied to the maternity board for a double license."

"You'll be fine, the doctors will fix you up in no time."

"You're a very bad liar, Murphy. I wish-"

The Hopper lurched and I jumped through the hatch without thinking.

"Cat? Chun?"

"Wasn't me, Murphy. Owwwww!" Cat limped around the Hopper. "I think I twisted my ankle when I fell."

"I touched the screen." Chun bounded over.

"And when you did, IT moved?"

Chun nodded.

"I'd guess IT's preparing to leave orbit. We didn't see it coming so its departure might be just as abrupt. Hell, we may have already left."

"Murphy? I feel strange..."

Cat keeled over. I reached out to catch her but found

105

myself falling too. The thump behind me had to be Chun. I could only lie helplessly on my side as a glowing blue mist filled the chamber. My mouth tasted like I'd been sucking on a power cell. Then I blacked out.

I jerked upright gasping, almost butting heads with Cat. My chest felt as if someone had been dancing on it and I realized that she'd given me CPR.

"Glad to see you're still with us, Murphy."

On a scale of one to ten where one is a genuine heart-felt smile and ten is completely forced, Cat's rated a twelve or thirteen.

"Glad to be here. Any idea where *here* is, by the way?" I looked around. "How are the others?"

"Chun is fine, he's checking on Devuyst."

As she spoke Chun emerged from the Hopper and raised his thumbs. Cat turned back to me.

"Was that some kind of space jump? What else could it be?"

Her suggestion fit the facts. IT had to be capable of superluminal flight and we knew from the start that it might move while we were inside it. It was reasonable to assume we were a long way from home.

"If we're at the IT homeworld, where are the owners? Shouldn't they be greeting us or something?" Chun frowned. "Maybe they have a different time perception; they may not know we're here yet."

"Or maybe they don't care," said Cat, stuffing her hands deep into her pockets.

"What kind of ship is this?" Maybe some debate would provide a distraction. "No crew from what we know. Probes create no reaction, but we trigger something in minutes. Flashing lights, those 'things' on the walls. Probes get in and out. But we get trapped?"

"Some kind of probe or sampling system?" Cat asked, scanning the entire room.

"To gather samples across interstellar distances?" Chun frowned. "That's crazy. Think of the time and resources needed to build it."

"How do we know what effort is involved?" I pointed around us. "This would be a huge commitment for us, but to them it could be trivial. Think about it. What do you do when you want to set up a trap? You make it attractive to the prey. You put in triggers to make sure it doesn't activate until you've caught something. If you're sampling intelligent life, what better bait than showing them other potential intelligence?"

"Even if you're right, Murph, it still doesn't make sense." Cat said. "Wouldn't they process us or something? We wouldn't take a sample and just ignore it."

I was going to say that people left animals in traps, sometimes till they died, but Chun pointed at the screen.

"Look!"

The pattern was fixed now and the background cycled between a sickly green and an almost equally repulsive shade of purple. The most interesting thing though was an entirely familiar "shape": the English word "Automatic."

"It's translating for us..." Chun's voice was hushed with childlike awe.

"That's not possible." I moved closer as another word appeared. "Does 'Krimanth' mean anything to anyone?"

The others shook their heads and I had to laugh. Maybe IT wasn't as smart as we'd given it credit for.

"IT needs our help," said Cat, ignoring my skepticism.

"Give it more words?" Chun pinched his chin. "Nice idea, but they likely have all the words we use. We'd need to supply context, but how? We don't know what things mean to IT."

"Charades?" Cat suggested.

"Anything is worth a try," I agreed.

"A condition or state that is dangerous or potentially damaging, this could lead to an Automatic reaction. Describes the situation when something fails or malfunctions."

"It's an emergency." Chun picked it up. "Something that

represents a wider group. One from many. You can use this to sample and compare..."

I'm not really sure how long we continued, but I was hoarse and Cat was red-eyed with fatigue. Even Chun, despite his initial excitement, was flagging and slouched against the wall.

The screen hadn't changed since the first two words. Then it blanked out completely before flashing three times. It cycled through a rainbow of different combinations until settling into a red and yellow pulsing, but there was still no message.

"Damn it!" I rubbed my forehead, trying to ease the pressure. My stress fuses were well and truly blown. Then I heard a bitter laugh and looked up.

"*This Xanzziflp automatic samples retrieve system has malfunctioning. Codes Q19753H - Warp Drive fails. Please return to Xanzziflp Products Division on Krimanth Four a consolation or otherwise optional grateful repayment.*"

"We're stuck? In a sample jar? Is this a joke?" Cat said.

"There must be something we can do. We have air, it doesn't seem to be running out. We're not done yet."

"Food? Water?" Chun glanced around. "There are limited supplies in the Hopper. Enough for a few days at most."

"We could take another look at the airlock. Maybe we could make it eject us." I didn't even convince myself.

"Where are we? Where's the nearest place we can dock with?" Cat's voice was now level and controlled. "The Hopper isn't built for atmospheric operations."

"There has to be something..." A half-forgotten weight hefted at my pocket and I pulled out the Lieutenant's pistol.

"Murphy!" Cat turned away, her features white.

"It might be for the best," Chun whispered. "What a choice — death by starvation, asphyxiation, or decompression. A bullet would be quick and relatively painless."

"Sorry. That's not an option." Devuyst clambered out of the Hopper, her face sweat-sheened and pasty. "The gun is keyed to my fingerprints for safety."

She held up her bandaged hands.
Cat's whistle was low. "Talk about Murphy's L-"
I jammed my fingers in my ears.

So there you have it. I'm recording this on the Hopper log system in hopes that somebody will find it one day. Will they understand this? Who knows. Will they be human? Unlikely. It's been two days since the message appeared and Chun believes he's managed to re-rig the quantum comm system to send a repeating broadcast. Bog knows who might pick it up.

Nobody will speak my name now. They always said it was a curse. I hope someone proves them wrong.

Soon.

The End

Humanity makes a great deal of use of sample capture and return systems. From simple systems that trap creatures to the complex ones used to return samples from the moon, comets and other planets. I wondered if an alien civilization more advanced than we are, might also use have the same idea. Like Murphy, I seem to have had a great deal of bad luck, despite trying to plan to avoid it. Mix together these two ideas and throw in a little military/civilian oil and water and Murphy's Law was born.

Reboot

Commissioner Bellarbi turned away from the reports and savored the earthy flavors of his herbal tea as he gazed at the majestic skyscrapers of the city skyline. Usually the subtly spiced drink was relaxing, but not today. After all, *she* was coming.

His screen flashed and Bellarbi touched the headline to bring up the details. Information was still sketchy, but it appeared that a nanotech production plant had been shut down due to corruption in the growth process.

Bellarbi tapped the comm patch and the boyish face of his secretary expanded to dominate the screen. "Myles? Is there any more on the Rekhavi case?"

"Only anecdotal reports so far, Commissioner." The secretary's voice held its usual practiced indifference. "Routine monitoring uncovered evidence that the materials were flawed and might interact with the environment in potentially dangerous, though as yet, undetermined ways."

"Why wasn't it discovered and corrected before becoming dangerous?"

"Presumably the correct monitoring procedures weren't followed. The plant operators claim otherwise, of course. Would you-"

Bellarbi flinched as a deafening blast of music came from

the speakers while the screen displayed a surreal abstract of jangling colors and shapes. "I didn't catch that Myles, these damn spikes get worse every day."

Myles reappeared. "I asked if I should assign a follow-up team."

A follow-up audit would be expensive and, as always, budgets were tight. Bellarbi's fingers drummed softly on the heavy polished desk. It would be hard to justify another intervention without clear evidence of damage or inappropriate behavior.

"Wait for the routine analysis." Bellarbi was about to cut off the transmission when he noticed something in Myles expression. "What is it?"

Myles paused, his mouth half open before speaking."There've been large street protests in London, New York, Madrid, Yokohama and Karachi, among others. I know you don't want to-

"You're right. I don't."

Bellarbi switched back to the summary view and brought up the monthly statistics. Incidents were up seventeen percent across the board on the previous month: communications, traffic control, industrial processing, and data systems. None seemed immune. Regardless of the origin, the infrastructure of society was being affected with an ever greater frequency and with it came an increase in social tensions. People were flooding the streets to protest what they saw of as signs of an uncaring bureaucracy content to let vital services and jobs be lost and he knew it wouldn't be long before there were public calls for his replacement.

The screen flashed again. "She's here, Commissioner."

Bellarbi felt a mix of relief and awe, but knew he couldn't let himself be intimidated. That would be a disaster given her reputation. "How... how is she?"

"That's hard to say," Myles glanced over his shoulder. "I don't think I've met anyone like her before."

"Pleased to meet you." Bellarbi jumped up as she entered, cursing silently at his graceless rush. "I hope you had a pleasant journey."

"Don't waste your breath on nonsense. I don't have the time at my age."

Maryum Casteneda bore scant resemblance to the pictures Bellarbi had seen. Generally she was depicted in severely efficient middle age, but the years since had thinned and sharpened her features. Despite that, her hair was still as carbon black as her piercing eyes.

"I assume something is wrong. I can't imagine anyone here being 'pleased' to see me otherwise." Casteneda perched on the unoccupied seat without waiting to be asked.

"Why would you say that? ISIA wouldn't exist without you. You're an honored guest and always welcome."

Casteneda glared at Bellarbi. "I'm an ancient crone who accidentally talked herself into a difficult job because no-one else had the intelligence to ask the right questions, or the nerve to deal with the answers. The Information Systems Investigation Authority was created for purely political motives."

Bellarbi drew a sharp breath. "The Authority is charged with the investigation of all inter-dependent systems-"

"'All inter-dependent systems in the light of failure or disruption, whether through accident, poor design or as a result of malicious human activity.' I know, I wrote it — now tell me something I don't know. Such as why it was necessary to drag an old woman away from her death bed."

"You're..?" Bellarbi couldn't finish.

"I have advanced lung cancer. The doctors have given me six months. I think less."

"What about regen-therapy? I'm sure you'd qualify with your background." Bellarbi shifted uneasily. He'd never been so close to someone seriously ill.

"Save the fake concern. That's not why you called me." Casteneda didn't bother to mention she'd checked herself out of the hospital because she couldn't stand the busy-bodying.

"You have a problem you can't handle or you wouldn't need me. Give me the details."

Bellarbi hesitated only briefly. "The first noticeable incident was the failure of Chicago City Transit: An automatic on-demand system designed to worked collaboratively with other transportation networks to ensure peak flow rates and–"

"I'm not a complete recluse. I heard the reports — for over thirty hours not a single iCab ran."

"It cost the city millions in lost revenue and compensation. Not to mention long term damage to the system's reputation." Bellarbi noted Casteneda's pained expression and hurried on. "Since then I've monitored a worrying rise in the number of serious failures. No discernible pattern or common cause I can identify, but it *is* happening. It's…"

Casteneda's tight-lipped silence made Bellarbi even more uncomfortable.

He sighed and opened his hands. "Sometimes it seems sinister, but tech-analysis always comes back negative on traces of wrongdoing. But I still feel there's some organization behind it. The Fundamentalists are always trying to stir up trouble."

"And men say women are superstitious." Casteneda snorted. "Faced with something you can't explain, you attribute it to malevolence rather than admit your limitations."

Bellarbi winced. "Perhaps you're right." He'd noticed a wheeze in her breathing and felt guilty. "There must be some explanation though; I've checked my search filter for flaws dozens of times."

"Then I better look smarter, rather than harder." Casteneda held out a metal fob. "Here's my Key. I want the highest available access on all systems."

He hesitated. With that, the old woman would be able to access every system, including information of the highest sensitivity. "I'm not sure–"

Casteneda stood abruptly and moved towards the door. "Call me when you change your mind."

"This is blackmail. I'll give you senior investigator status

114

— you can't expect more."

"You contacted me, remember." With that she was gone.

Bellarbi gripped the edge of his heavy desk, the smooth oak cold under his hands. Casteneda had a reputation for being difficult, but he wasn't prepared for this prima donna attitude. Technical staff always had a pronounced "will do" approach and, as ex-ISIA, he'd expected her to be the same.

It had been a mistake to call her in; what could she do anyway? She was a dinosaur — a relic of a dead age that didn't really fit in the complexity of the modern world. She'd even publicly criticized the Agency when they'd dropped the requirement for traditional Information Theory skills from its recruitment program. *He* managed to run the department perfectly well without such a qualification.

The screen flashed as another report came in. Details were few. Monitoring systems had failed in the California vineyard complexes and, whatever the cause, the estimated cost ran into millions.

He slapped the edge of the screen, realizing he still held Casteneda's personal data Key. "Myles, get hold of that woman again; she's probably half way home by now but I don't care. Get her back, even if you have to drag her by the neck."

The secretary frowned and a few moments later the screen border flashed green indicating Myles had activated the hush shield. "I don't understand, Commissioner. Ms. Casteneda has been in the waiting room for the last ten minutes."

Bellarbi handed over the Key, his jaw tight. "You should have everything you need."

"I'm glad you came to your senses." Casteneda's breathing sounded more labored. "Now get out and let me work."

"I'd like to stay, if you don't mind. It's possible I can help."

"Do you have any knowledge of low-level execution threads, network trace partitioning and Q-Crypt transmission protocols?" Casteneda paused. "I thought as much, you're a political appointee like the others who came after me."

"I'll be outside. Let me know if I can help with anything." Bellarbi's last shreds of defiance crumbled.

"Wait. There *is* something you can do." Casteneda didn't look up as Bellarbi span back. "Fetch me a jug of coffee, at least a liter. And none of that caffeine-free dishwater."

Casteneda plugged her Key into the user port and waited a few seconds while the terminals reconfigured to her access. She had her own way of working and wouldn't have the willpower to start if she had to configure everything manually and install all her tools. Many of them had been specially written by her and refined through over fifty years of use. Popping open the main diagnostic and trace systems had a comfortable feeling to it and momentarily she forgot how long it had been. She wondered idly if they'd been used since she'd left and if anyone would use them after she died.

She smiled grimly. "They probably wouldn't understand them anyway."

Casteneda started checking basic large-scale indicators. Decades earlier, she'd created specialized low-level monitoring data Sinks in a number of key systems, none authorized. She hoped she'd buried them deep enough to remain hidden. If enough were still active, she should see cascade effects from the current array of problems — which might provide a back door to the cause.

While waiting for the Sinks to report, Casteneda brought up Bellarbi's incident search. Skimming through the results told her that the Commissioner had grounds for concern. Nevertheless she took nothing for granted; even the best analysis could be flawed.

The office door opened and Bellarbi skulked in, carrying a large coffee pot and a plate of assorted sweet pastries. Casteneda couldn't help but smile as he placed them in front of her. "I'm sorry to say that your search algorithm is correct." Casteneda helped herself to the strong black coffee, adding a significant amount of sugar.

Bellarbi stiffened. "Was there some doubt?"

"Yes." Casteneda glanced up when Bellarbi didn't leave. "I'm not going to find the answer in ten minutes and I don't need you hovering at my elbow. What's more, I won't protect your job, if there's incompetence behind these incidents I'll tell the world."

Bellarbi looked like he'd been slapped, but turned and trudged back through the door. Casteneda sighed. For a moment she'd thought Bellarbi would simply refuse and she'd have to put up with him. She didn't always work strictly by the book and he would only have argued with her.

A soft ping drew her attention to the screen. She was surprised; seventy-three percent of the Sinks were still intact. None had been accessed in over twenty years and the size of the audit logs meant it would take some time to catalog in her summary tools.

"You boys haven't been cleaning out the trash," she murmured.

Two more jugs of coffee and over thirteen hours passed before Bellarbi saw the summons flash on his secretary's screen. Myles had long since left and the Commissioner had dozed in his secretary's chair. He stood and stretched, trying to relieve the cramp in his back.

Casteneda was slumped over the console when Bellarbi entered and momentarily he wondered if she was dead. He couldn't help thinking about how inconvenient the press coverage would be and how many reports he'd have to complete.

Casteneda dragged her head up as he approached. Her dark eyes were sunken caves, but she managed a weak smile, though somehow that made her seem smaller and more helpless.

"Don't worry." Casteneda tapped the screen. "I've finished."

Bellarbi swallowed hard at his thoughts just moments before.

"You look… ill." It was a stupid response and he waited for the inevitable barbed reply.

"I feel ill too." Castenedas laugh was more a wet choke. "It doesn't matter anymore."

"I'll call an ambulance."

"Listen." The dominant Casteneda resurfaced. "You need to understand."

Bellarbi sat down, guilt and concern smothering his objections.

"How many discrete information systems are there in the world?"

Bellarbi shook his head. "We have rough estimates. Hundreds of millions certainly, billions possibly."

"The usual presumption, but wrong." Casteneda struggled upright. "There's just one."

"But, that's imp-"

"All the systems are linked in some way; nothing is truly independent. Before retiring, I ran a Seiler topological analysis, tracing the connective complexity in the systems. I just tried to run one again and it couldn't complete in over ten hours. The results I did get back indicated that the complexity is now over a billion times higher."

"Everything, from the backbone services and core memory vats, to the smallest personal system are linked so tightly it's impossible to map all the connections. Anyone with criminal intentions can get to any system from any point world-wide. If they were sufficiently skilled, it would be virtually untraceable despite the built-in security protocols."

Bellarbi fingered the bristles on his chin. If Casteneda was right, then the potential danger was far higher than ISIA was prepared for. There was no way to know where the terrorists would strike next. "Have you isolated the source of the attacks?"

"You still don't understand." Casteneda gripped his wrist with surprising strength. "There have been no attacks. The system itself is failing. We've increased interconnections and embedded technology into *everything*. It's a gigantic technical tower built on foundations suitable for a wooden shack. It doesn't need outside help to fail."

Bellarbi drew back. Why, she's almost anti-tech, he thought. "Is there anything we can do?"

"Shut it down." Casteneda whispered. "Restart everything. With luck the systems will synchronize properly as they come back on-line. I've programmed a route-trace macro that will work through every system, re-factoring and reinforcing the foundations when it's executed. Like an old style virus. But you need to do it offline." Her short laugh was harsh.

Casteneda was fading even as Bellarbi watched. He moved closer. Her eyes flickered slightly as he took her hand but her skin was cold against his.

"Wait, what do we restart? The Data Spine? The Core?"

Casteneda's breathing was a faint rasp. "Everything. Need..." her words barely audible. "...shut it all down..."

Bellarbi hit the comm patch. "I need a MedTech team — now!"

He cradled Casteneda in his arms to prevent her from falling. Shut down everything? That was impossible. It would be like... He struggled to find a suitable comparison. Like restarting the world. He stared at the flashing button on his screen. The word meant nothing to him.

"Reboot."

The End

My career background is in technology. I started out as a software developer, then moved on to systems and business analysis, then into project management. One of the issues I see is our increasing reliance on technology and the way we are — purely for convenience — linking systems that probably shouldn't be. Extrapolate that and you end up with systems so linked that they essentially become just one. Not only that, any system that grows in such an "organic" fashion is going to become increasingly and unpredictably unreliable. Imagine the entire world powered by Windows 95!

Version Control

"I didn't V-Up this week," Mel Culter whispered, before delivering another forkful of string beans to her exquisitely shaped mouth.

Dan wasn't listening closely. He slipped his hand inside his pocket and pinched the two tickets tightly, the plastic diamonds cold against his skin. "The Strones are playing at the Arena next weekend. It's nearly impossible to get tickets, but well, I have a friend and-"

"Danny Gill, you're not paying attention." Mel crossed her arms and thumped back in her chair. "That's two weeks."

"Are you crazy?" Dan finally realized what she'd said and glanced around. The only other people in the lunch room were two tables away and had their heads down ignoring the flickering advertising surfaces that covered the walls. "You could lose your job for that."

"Only if they find out." Mel hesitated. She'd known Danny for three years ever since starting at Magleby's on the same day. They'd become friends through that need, common to new recruits, for an ally. "You wouldn't tell on me, would you?"

Dan pushed the tickets back deep in his pocket. That was the last thing he would have done. Despite his feelings, Mel often worried him. She sometimes had wild ideas and this one ended in only two ways: Career Freeze with no promotion or increment for at least five year,s or getting sent back to the Assignment Center with zero priority.

"It's stupid." Mel's fork clattered onto her plate. "Why do we have to pay to work in a job anyway? Especially one going nowhere."

"How else would you know what to do? The systems? Company policies and procedures?" Dan tapped the metal disk of the MemPlant behind his ear. "Without this you'd have to spend years learning everything. You know how things change all the time."

"Who says it would take years?"

"Everybody knows." The always slightly fetid smell in the canteen irritated his nose and he wiped it carefully with a tissue, not wanting to blow it in front of Mel. "How'd you manage it anyway?"

"That's what *they* tell you. I flipped digits on my account code. Listen, I was reading a book I found in my parents' stuff..."

"Yeah, right..." Dan chuckled, immediately regretting it when Mel frowned.

"Listen, Mr. Hole-In-Brain, my grandmother taught me how to read the old-fashioned way. She used to be an actual librarian."

Dan held up his hands in surrender. He should have known better, but no-one spent days or weeks trying to learn stuff from books anymore. You paid your subscription and everything you needed to know was available in a second through the MemPlant.

"The book said at one time everyone read and learned things for themselves. They didn't have MemPlants and they still got jobs and everything."

"There's lots of things people *used* to do. Like living in caves and hunting animals to eat. Or living in pyramids." He crumpled up the plastic cup and dropped it on his plate for disposal. "Someone once told me in olden days they used to clean their yeenies with their hands, but would you? We don't do those things now because it's not civilized." Dan cut himself off, he didn't want Mel to think he was unsympathetic.

"That is so gross. With their hands? Yuch. I'm still eating." Mel crunched the last of her beans. "Do you want to hear this?"

Dan would have listened to Mel no matter what she wanted to talk about, but never managed to tell her that. Again he thought about the tickets. "Mel, I was wondering... never mind, tell me."

"It's so expensive. They've put up the price three times this month alone. It's getting to the point where it's hardly worth working at all. It's like we're going backwards. Remember when we first started? I signed up for that subscription on Scientific Business Management. Had to give it up, can't afford it."

"Do you think you'd be better off on subsistence tokens and zero health credits?" Dan regretted it immediately when Mel glared at him, the light from the mass of displays around them reflecting in her eyes like burning flames.

"The book said people learned what they needed themselves and it made me think. Wouldn't people be more flexible and creative if they did that? Everyone would see things a little different. It wouldn't be just the same-old-shinkers. I'm sure I could run this place as well as old Magleby, maybe better. When was the last time the company introduced a new product line?"

Dan shook his head. The R & D team only seemed to produce more variants of the same product lines. Bigger surfaces maybe, a few more tweaks to the attention recognition software, but that was about it. His gaze lingered on the screens behind Mel for too long and they immediately reacted to his inadvertent attention and accessed his personal marketing profile, splashing the walls with a series of lurid dating ads. He looked back at Mel, hoping she hadn't noticed.

But Mel was still deep in her own thoughts. "Think about it. If you got stuck, you'd figure out how to solve it yourself. Not just do what the MemPlant tells you." Mel chewed the inside of her cheek. "Work would be fun and then people could improve and get better jobs by working hard, not just because they can pay."

Dan noticed Mel was breathing faster, her face slightly flushed as she talked. It made his skin tingle, but what she was saying was just nuts.

"Look around, Mel. Do you see anyone looking for 'flexible' people? Do you see a pile of vacancies for creative people? Have you ever heard of people having fun at work? Of course not, because it doesn't exist. That's the sort of fluffy nonsense you'd see in a kids' show, right alongside unicorns, elves and the handsome Prince." He squirmed slightly, hoping Mel wouldn't rile up at his comments. "That's not all though. Where would you get all these books from? I've only ever seen them in museums and on 3V shows. Not to mention that the information would be out of date."

"You could learn the principles and then adapt to new situations."

"What about certification? If you learned everything there was to know about being, say a brain surgeon, that doesn't make you qualified to operate on people. You can't just claim you know something, you have to be able to prove it."

"They tested people, made them prove they learned it."

"What does that show? What if someone cheated? What if they learned something then forgot it? It would be a complete waste of time."

"It's *not* a waste. I learned the last two week's updates without the V-Up. I'm still on version 2017.451.095," Mel hissed. "I did it by watching the other women. You know there wasn't hardly anything different."

"Oh jeez. Mel? What are you doing?" Dan checked his MemPlant. "You're not two Vs behind, you're three!"

"Sure. But I know everything just the same." Mel was annoyed; she'd expected Dan to understand if anyone would. She'd got the idea that maybe he wanted to be more than friends, but he'd never once dropped even a hint and now she wondered if he just wasn't interested. "And I haven't had to *pay* for the last three either."

Dan rubbed his fingers against the rough plastic tabletop. He worked in Quality Control and when he thought about it, he couldn't remember any real changes in his own work. It was a dull routine with almost mind-numbing petty detail variations. But that was probably because of the lack of product innovation.

"What if you *don't* know it all? What if there's something not obvious and you miss it. You could be fired for improper procedure maintenance." He suddenly felt the urge to escape, if only temporarily, to gather his thoughts. "I need a drink - want one?"

Mel nodded and he shuffled over to the vending machine. Checking that the Orange juice had three heart icons he paid for two through his MemPlant. Mel always insisted on the "three heart" healthy option, so he did too. The drinks were frosty enough to make his fingertips prickle as he carried them back and set them down on the table.

Mel leaned closer as he sat back down, her voice even quieter than earlier. "There's something else, Dan."

Dan groaned. What else could there be? "Listen, Mel. If it's a problem, I'll let you have the credits to pay. I should have enough." He wondered how much the Strones tickets would sell for, not as much as he'd paid that was certain.

"Don't be silly. Listen to me though. Dan, what if they limit what they tell us? Maybe they *don't* tell us everything."

"Sure they do." Dan was confused. "That's why we pay the subscription."

"What if you wanted more than this?" Mel spun her finger in the air. "What then?"

"Then I'd hope I came from a rich family so I could pay the V-Ups, of course. Or you could save like crazy and buy them yourself I guess." Dan shrugged. "I don't understand."

"The way things are, we're going to do this forever. There's no way we can move up because they don't give us enough information. We're just office slaves and that's all we'll ever be.

And why do the V-Ups cost so much?"

Mel slurped her juice. "I've got a friend. He works over at Tren-Hump Cortical. He told me that the V-Ups cost next to nothing. It's a bunch of standard programs. The same for everyone in each job type. So the cost of producing them gets split over thousands of people."

"A friend?" Dan suddenly felt very unhappy.

"Sure. What of it?"

"Nothing." Dan crunched the orange carton into a twisted mess. "Did he say how much?"

"Less than a buck each."

Dan couldn't believe it. He'd paid over three hundred for V-Ups the last month alone and they'd told him the fees were going up the next time.

"What if I wanted to be a pilot?" said Mel. "Between rent, eating, and V-Ups there's not much left over - I could never afford that."

"Then you should probably have been born to parents who were pilots. Or maybe join the military. That's always an option."

"And you don't see anything wrong with that?"

Mel was breathing heavily and Dan sensed her frustration. Yes, it was boring and mindless. But it was better than being out of work. By a long way. Without a job there was no health protection, you lived on subsistence tokens that could only be exchanged for the very barest of essentials (unless you went to an illegal token dealer), and lived in Community dorms. At least working you could buy a few comforts.

"Who is this anonymous 'they' anyway?" he asked. "Are you talking about some kind of conspiracy? The V-Ups are managed by the government. They have inspectors and controls to make sure everything is legitimate. They wouldn't let it be abused. How would that benefit them?"

"I don't know. But just imagine if you taught yourself. Nothing could stop you. You could do anything, *be* anything you wanted. There'd be nothing to stop you. You'd be free to do anything. Don't you see?"

"Maybe. I guess..." Dan wondered how it would feel, someone like him becoming a pilot or space-ship engineer.

Mel's supervisor stuck her head through the door. "Lunch finished three minutes ago. You should be back at your stations."

"Yes, Ms. Razo," Mel and Dan chorused.

Ms. Razo paused, checking her MemPlant. "Mel, you're off accounts processing and assigned to general duties. Please ensure you V-Up before the end of the week or it may be permanent - or worse. I'm also warning your supervisor to keep a close eye on you, Mr. Gill."

Mel's shoulders sagged. "Yes, Ms. Razo."

They hurried from the canteen. Mel turned left at the first corner and Dan started to turn towards the testing labs, then stopped.

"Mel?" Dan pulled the tickets out of his pocket, the holographic surfaces glittering in the meager light that managed to fight through the grimy windows. "About the Strones?"

"Sure, Dan. We can go I guess." She kept her back to him, not wanting him to see her tears of frustration and defeat.

"And Mel?" Dan stepped closer, his voice dropping to a whisper. "Maybe after, we could read some of your books together?"

Mel's heart seemed to swell inside her chest and she smiled back at Dan before hurrying down the corridor.

The End

David M. Kelly

This is another piece of "flash fiction". At work everyone is expected to keep up to date with all the latest technology and processes as well as being "certified" even if the certification is meaningless and provides nothing more than a check-mark on a manager's list. At the same time, companies and organizations don't want to pay for their staff to go on training, they don't want to give people time to train or even support them by giving them time for self-learning. Combine this with the ever-increasing trend toward "pay to play" and the cell-phone model of business and we have this story. This was another one I essentially dreamt, waking up with the whole thing pretty much fully-formed.

A Slight Imperfection

Alec Myre dragged the old-fashioned wet razor down the left side of his neck and stopped. For a second he saw a mark there, a slight whitening of the skin a few millimeters across. He scoffed at his moment of paranoia and went back to shaving, only to stop again almost immediately.

No—he *wasn't* going crazy. There was another mark on the opposite side of his neck, a mirror image of the first. The marks were barely noticeable, but he was extra sensitive after last night's documentary on cancer.

Downstairs Elisha was in the airy kitchen placing steaming buttered toast on the pine table, but she immediately noticed his concern and stopped.

"What's wrong, Alec?"

"There are a couple of unusual marks on my neck. Would you take a look?" He sat down.

"You think it's serious?" Elisha leaned over him, peering at his skin as if intensity of vision was enough to reveal any problem.

"Do you see them? Tiny white marks."

"No, uhh, maybe…" She brushed her finger against the back of his neck, a gesture she knew he loved. "Does that help?"

Alec sighed. "You do pick your moments."

She smiled, her fine eyebrows arching. "Danny's over at

the Fredrics' for the morning. We have the place to ourselves."

"Dammit, I'm serious about this." Alec took a long breath. "Do you see the marks or not? Two little white spots, slightly indented or flattened maybe."

"No—don't see them. Can you point to them?"

Alec raised his finger and ran it over the general area; there was nothing there, just smooth skin and the gentle bristle of newly shaved skin. No, there! There *was* something; he could feel the indentation just slightly. He felt the other side of his neck and quickly found the matching spot.

"There, do you see where I am touching?"

Elisha looked closely, tilting her head this way and that to get a better view, pursing her lips in extreme concentration. "I really don't see anything that looks unusual."

"You're just not looking properly." Alec tugged on the skin more. "There! It's a different color. Don't you see?"

"Oh Alec, it's just a little difference. You're a scientist. You know that people's skin isn't uniform."

"That doesn't explain why there's *exactly* the same spot in the same place on the opposite side."

Elisha ruffled his hair. "You are such a silly thing sometimes. I'm sure it's not *really* identical." Her face grew serious. "Are you working too hard? I know things aren't easy at the lab."

"We're trying to understand some of the most fundamental processes of nature; it's never going to be easy." Alec frowned; he knew he sounded bombastic at times despite trying not to. "But I'm not cracking up, if that's what you mean."

"Perhaps you should speak with a Guide?"

Elisha did her best to make the question as inconsequential as possible, but it rankled Alec. The suggestion was always there when he became passionate about something, no matter how rational his arguments were.

Have you spoken to a Guide? Talk to the Guides, I'm sure they can help. As if his mental stability was so low it needed bolstering at every slight problem. There'd only been that one time: years ago now, but that was enough. The "low mental resilience" designation had been pinned firmly to him for life. He couldn't stop his anger spilling out. "Why do you bring that up? Do *you* think there's something wrong with me?"

Elisha reached for Alec, but he pulled back. "No, of course not. It's just…"

"Just what? That you think I'm useless? That I can't cope?"

"Don't bite my head off." Elisha's voice was sharp, but then softened. "I'm just trying to look after you."

"I'm okay. Don't worry about me."

His tone was bitter and Alec regretted it immediately. He sighed. Elisha was trying to help and he knew that. He just wished she wasn't so intent on trying to cocoon him.

"Are we sure about these figures?" Shumena Himmons played idly with the transparent Flimsy she held in front of her, not paying much attention to the words and numbers scrolling up the sheet.

She'd been director of the lab for over fifteen years. In that time Alec had watched her transform from master cosmologist, at the head of her field, into a somewhat competent bureaucrat. Now she was buried under a mountain of picayune duties with no time to stay current on the latest developments.

Alec hesitated. "You doubt my analysis?"

"We're scientists, Alec. An analysis may be perfect—but the conclusions cansometimes be biased."

"These aren't wild claims, Dr. Himmons." Alec straightened in his chair. "My work has been checked several times by different researchers. My theory has held up under the closest scrutiny."

"So after decades of accepting Dark Energy and all its consequences, we should just throw it out because of a few pieces of rogue data? Let a slight imperfection destroy the work of the greatest minds of our time?"

Alec always felt intimidated in Himmons' lavish office. Her desk was so wide and meticulously clean, unlike his own cluttered lab. He wasn't about to be muzzled though and stood up. "Sometimes a slight imperfection is all that's needed to disprove something. The effect of Dark Energy has been massively overstated. My research shows the actual value is less than ten percent of the generally accepted figure."

"And as a result the Universe will eventually halt its expansion and collapse back on itself in the exact opposite of the Big Bang?"

"Yes, completing this part of the cycle."

Dr. Himmons peered up at him, her eyeglasses catching the light so that they looked like an impassable silver mirror.

"This cycle?"

"My reports are not..." Alec hesitated. "Not fully complete. I have data I haven't released yet."

"Scientists don't withhold information." The mirrored lenses flashed. "Especially from their-"

"I appreciate it's unusual, but so are the circumstances. I've extended my analysis beyond the eventual collapse and can show that not only does it happen, but that it's a vital step in the rebirth of the Universe. The Universe is cyclical."

"Cyclical? That's ancient nons-"

"Cyclical. Infinite. And this is not the first cycle." Alec paused for Himmons to take in what he was saying. "I've measured trace echoes of at least three previous Universes overlaid on ours. Nothing dies forever."

Alec felt as if he were floating above the chair. He'd finally been able to tell someone what he'd found. The release of his secret made him feel exhilarated and light-headed.

"How could you... it's impossible..." Himmons hesitated briefly, then placed her glasses precisely centered on the desk before her. "Alec, I'm not usually one for encouraging informality—perhaps that's a mistake. But I'm not a complete robot either. I spoke to Elisha earlier."

"Elisha?" Alec swallowed hard.

"She called and mentioned you were worried about some spots you'd found. I understand you were quite... agitated about it."

"I thought there were some marks on my skin and I was worried they might be serious." Alec looked away briefly. "It was nothing, just 3V-inspired paranoia."

"Elisha seemed quite worried."

Alec didn't reply. Anything he could say right now would just make things sound worse, but inside he burned. How could Elisha go behind his back like this? She'd disrespected him and betrayed him to one of his colleagues—and the Director of all people.

"I'd like you to see a Guide." Himmons held up a hand to forestall Alec's protest. "I'm not saying there's anything wrong with you and this has no bearing on the, uhh, theory you've presented."

"But as your employer we have a duty to ensure your well-being, Alec. I'm sure if one of your junior researchers was in similar circumstances, you'd suggest the same."

First Elisha, now Himmons. "Are you ordering me to?"

"Of course not. This is a research institute, not a military establishment."

"How was it Alec?"

Elisha greeted him at the door with her usual smile, though Alec knew it was forced. A wall had built up between them. Her betrayal still left him unable to respond to her other than with cordial neutrality. It felt like their relationship had ended the moment he'd left Himmons' office.

He shrugged. "The usual. The Guide's convinced my theories stem from the trauma of losing my parents and a psychotic need to prove they're not really dead. I'm apparently 'fixated' on the concept that the universe will be reborn and them with it."

"Does he really call you psychotic?"

"I suppose that's my translation. He just talks about 'contacting my inner feelings' and 'releasing suppressed grief'. He doesn't see the spots on my neck either." Alec slumped on the sofa. Just thinking about the Guide angered him and he wanted to wanted to change the subject. "Where's Danial?"

"He's playing at the Fredrics'. It's so good that we have a neighbor with a boy a similar age. I don't know how we'd cope without them."

"We help them too. Jimmy comes around here a lot."

"I know. I was just thinking though, wouldn't it be nice if we had someone else for Dan to play with. Maybe a little sister? Don't you think?"

Alec stiffened as Elisha brushed her fingertips across his cheek, snuggling close in to him.

"I don't think…"

"Then don't then." Elisha's lips were warm on his.

Alec wrenched himself away. "You're unbelievable. You think you can make up for everything by doing that?"

Elisha reddened. "No Alec, I just w-"

"How could you even think about having another child? We're not exactly a couple anymore."

"Don't say that. I still love you."

"And that's why you turned me in to the Director…" Alec stalked away to his office

"Alec?" Elisha whispered through the part-opened door. "I'm sorry. I didn't mean it to be how you thought."

His temper had died, leaving Alec feeling exhausted and ashamed as it always did. "The timing isn't good, that's all."

Elisha slipped through the door carrying a small tray of coffee and some of his favorite cookies. "I thought you might like these."

"Peace offering?" Alec grunted, but took a bite from a cookie.

"Just saying sorry."

"What makes you so sure that things have happened before?" Elisha sat in the upholstered chair a few feet way. "Surely it's impossible to tell."

Alec sipped his coffee, he didn't want to talk about it but maybe it would distract her from more uncomfortable subjects.

"There's an imperfection in the background data."

"What imperfection?"

"It's a little complicated." He struggled to sit up. "Are you sure you want to know?"

"I want to understand." Elisha's jaw set. "I'm not empty-headed."

Alec sighed. "Okay… according to standard theory, Dark Energy is pushing everything apart. I looked at the data, but the evidence didn't show enough of it existed to cause that, so I started looking for other explanations."

"Without enough Dark Energy there's nothing pushing things apart and eventually gravity will become the dominant force in the Universe. Everything will fly towards the gravitational center and squish together into a space smaller than a subatomic particle. You still with me?"

Elisha glared at him. "I understand English. Even yours."

Alec raised his coffee cup to her. "When I analyzed cosmic background radiation, I found very subtle traces of previous organizations of matter."

"You lost me there."

"Imagine it's like a piece of paper and you write a note on it. Later you erase it, but there will still be traces, no matter how hard you try. Tiny fragments and remnants survive and, with sufficiently powerful analysis, they can be recovered."

"You found that?" Elisha sounded pleased, "It must have been very difficult."

"The data is absolutely clear to anyone who looks with an unbiased mind. The fact is that there have been several previous Universes, each one rebuilt on top of the old one."

"That's incredible." Elisha leaned forward and smiled, but this time it seemed genuine. "You'll soon be famous. I better start looking for a frock for the Nobel ceremony."

"Don't get carried away. The Lab has put a hold on publication of my results."

"It's probably only temporary. Is it a problem if they don't support you?"

It was a question Alec had thought about for several weeks. This wasn't the old days when you could publish without the backing of an institute. Although he could publish independently to a wide audience, that would risk his position and reputation. Even if things weren't the best between him and Elisha, he still had family responsibilities.

"I'm not sure. It would definitely be awkward. I could lose my place at the lab. Maybe it doesn't matter to anyone, even if I'm right. We're talking about an event that won't happen for billions of years."

"But if it's true, then people should know." Elisha moved across and squeezed Alec's hand with surprising firmness. "You should do what's right."

"Mom! Dad!" Danial bawled from the lower floor.

"I'll go." Elisha gave him a quick kiss and left.

The kiss felt nice. Alec felt a little guilty that he'd enjoyed it and tried to focus on publishing instead. He could set up a site, present his findings. It wouldn't cost much. Or maybe use a free service. No, that would make him look more like a crackpot. If he did, then just m...

"Alec, please come down."

Elisha's voice sounded strange. It drifted into his office as though whispered, even though he knew there was anxiety behind it.

A few minutes later he bolted upright. He'd still been thinking about publishing and the repercussions. Elisha had called and he'd heard nothing since. Alec ran downstairs, tumbling down the last few stairs and catching his elbow painfully on the floor.

A faint golden glow drifted through the air, as if it were fog rather than a light effect—like the flow from the morning sun carried on a mist of ether. The glow thickened towards the kitchen and Alec scrabbled to the doorway, bare feet squeaking on the tiled floor.

Elisha stood on one side of the room with her arm protectively around Danial. Her head was lowered so Alec couldn't see her face, but he sensed that neither of them was breathing. They were motionless as if frozen. His stomach churned. He tried to move towards them, but his legs seemed paralysed.

The glow brightened to his right, coalescing into a shapeless turbulence of light that burned his eyes and pulsed as if alive. Alec heard a loud deafening heartbeat, but knew it was inside his head not external.

Alec stared at Elisha and Danial. "Why?"

The streams of light imploded in waves like a golden whirlpool, the center brightening until the whole kitchen faded from sight. Then in a snap the light disappeared, leaving behind a man in a dark-blue casual suit.

"Hello, Alec."

"Who are you?" Alec trembled, realizing the figure was identical to his high-school math teacher; impossible unless the teacher had been frozen in time for over twenty years.

"I'm from *Outside*." The figure hesitated. "Would you accept it if I said I'm God?"

"No." Alec tried to move towards Elisha again but couldn't. It was a strange paralysis. He could move his head and speak, but he was pinned in place. "If that's the best you can do, you better try again."

"Would it be more acceptable if I said I was an alien visitor?"

Alec shook his head. "I'm a scientist. Give me proof."

The figure shivered, his outline blurring momentarily with a burning light brighter than anything Alec had ever seen. "I'm a mathematician." The figure smiled. "Much like you."

"What have you done to them?" Tears rolled down Alec's cheeks. "Whatever you want, please don't hurt them."

"Don't be upset. They are unharmed. They can't be in fact." Again the figure hesitated as though finding it difficult communicating. "We're not evil."

"Who is 'we'?"

"Those of us… Outside."

"Outside where?"

"None of this is real, Alec. I'm the creator." The figure stumbled. "That is I… We, made all of this."

"That's impossible." Alec shook his head. "I'm real. They're real. *This* is real. Why are you lying? What do you really want?"

"We run tests—like you do in your research. Everything you know is a complex simulation. We wanted to test how life and intelligence developed on its own. Some of us think that intelligence is inevitable, others think it a rarity. We could never find the answer before."

Alec snorted. Even if they could recreate the level of complexity and detail in the world, it would take far too long. Who'd start a project knowing it would take billions of years to get the results?

The figure seemed to share Alec's thoughts. "Our timescale is different from yours. It's one of the things that makes communication so difficult."

"So why this visit?"

The figure flickered again, briefly changing shape between his schoolteacher, Dr. Himmons, and the Guide.

"This is very hard. In fact we've never tried it before."

Alec felt his temper flare. "I'm sorry we've caused you so much inconvenience…"

The figure moved closer to Alec, seeming to study him intently. "We made an error and now it's threatening to destroy our work. *You* are threatening it."

"Like you, when we run our simulations, we don't just run it once but hundreds or thousands of times to get accurate results."

"That's what we've done; you exist in cycle 11,394 of the current series of simulations. Each time we wipe out all traces of the previous simulations entirely, or that's what we thought. Somehow some minute traces were left, which you noticed. We hadn't allowed for that."

"Even if that's true, why me? Why would I notice rather than someone else?"

"That's a good question. And we don't really have the answer. In this cycle we recast some relatively minor intellectual sequences in order to match what we thought we knew about how intelligence developed. There shouldn't have been any significant difference in the outcome at your epoch, but then you started to see patterns that you shouldn't. Like the marks on your neck."

"We make things as detailed as possible, but the marks represent the limits of our Holix engines. Programming them out would be expensive and our budgets aren't unlimited. We hid them as best we could, but it was another flaw in our processes I'm afraid."

Alec wanted to punch the figure to the ground. He could squeeze his hands into tight fists, but was still helplessly frozen. A simulation? What nonsense. He might as well believe in fairies or pixies if that were true.

"You won't get away with this. Whatever you're planning, I'll…"

"We don't have time for this, Alec. Your releasing information about the nature of your universe is already polluting the simulation; we have to clean it up before it spreads too far. Your wife and child, along with your colleagues have had all knowledge of this purged from their minds. Imagine it's like a disease, spreading through healthy tissue from the site of infection. If we act now we might be able to stop it before it becomes too costly, but the longer it goes on the harder it is to contain and the greater the chance that this entire sequence will have to be abandoned."

Alec twisted and fell, squirming like a worm on the floor. "Even if it's true, why not just wipe *my* mind too? If I'm just a piece in a simulation, what do you care? Just wipe my mind too and get on with it."

"Well…"

"Ah! Your ideas fall apart at the first rational inspection. You've drugged me and my family for some reason and…"

"Alec." The figure reached down and lifted him back up,

placing him on a kitchen stool as if he were made of nothing. "Look at your wife's neck."

"No!" Alec tried to struggle further. "I won't believe… whatever you've done…" Despite himself, his eyes were drawn towards Elisha. "It's not true. It can't be."

"We have a special interest in you Alec; you're one of the central strands we are examining closely. If we modify you, this cycle would become worthless and undermine all our other work. We want to avoid that, but we can't do it without your help."

"What do you mean?"

"We need you to agree not to pursue your current research. Discuss your theories of the cyclical Universe with no one."

"The people I've told won't remember?"

"You're the only person who knows about your work now."

"What about my family?" Alec's glanced at his wife then looked back. "Will I still be with them?"

"That won't change. You will live out your life as normal."

Alec dragged in raw lungfuls of air, his eyes screwed into clenched slits. "What happens if I don't? What's the 'or else'?"

"Alec, we don't want this… that's why I came to you like this. We're not evil…"

"What will happen?" Alec screamed.

"We would have to eliminate the source of the infection to ensure there was full containment. Your wife and child would believe you had a regrettable accident."

Tears streamed down Alec's face and neck. "You can't ask me to do that. It would be…"

The figure flickered again, the light streaming from his profile in streams of impossible fire.

"We're out of time, Alec. Decide now."

"There's Daddy!" Danial's shout was clear all the way across the park and Alec smiled. Seconds later his arms were full of little boy and he swung the youngster into the sky, eliciting squeals of pleasure.

Elisha sauntered over and slid her arms around both of them, the three of them holding tight on to one another. The air was suffused with the smell of fresh grass and not even an insect disturbed the warm spring evening.

Alec gripped her tightly. "I love you."

Elisha squeezed him back. "How are things at the Lab?"

Alec hesitated imperceptibly. "You know, the usual routine. It's good to get home to you two." His eyes slipped away, deliberately avoiding the small discoloration on his wife's neck.

It was such a slight imperfection.

The End

This one had very strange beginnings. I was getting ready for work one morning and doing my ritual shave when I noticed a little white patch of skin just on the side of my neck where I could barely see it. When I started on the other side of my face I noticed an almost identical patch. I mentioned it to my wife and she said she couldn't see anything, but the seed was planted.

Of course, the marks weren't really identical like Alec's, at least I don't think... Hang on, I just want to check something...

First Contact

"This is a screw-up of the highest order. The goddammed 'Evil Alien Syndrome' made real."

Al Ortiz paced around the burl wood veneered desk, plowing his fingers through his thick hair. The tension throbbed in his temples. No one could possibly have guessed *this* would happen and not only that, but live on 3V with thousands of "in-person" witnesses.

Dan Guzik whirled his finger in space and let out a low whistle. "The Agency is nuts if they think we can sit on this."

Ortiz slumped into a padded chair, the scent of leather and polish enveloping him. Guzik was right. The feeds on his phone already showed multiple copies of the original feed being uploaded, downloaded, and watched. Less than one hour after the incident, it had gone viral. Shutting it down would be like battling a legendary hydra — every time they killed one feed a dozen more would spring up.

Ortiz checked the time, his square jaw clenching and un-clenching. "Are you *sure* she's coming?"

"I just told ya. Everything's jammed up — it'll take a while."

It should have been a triumph of interstellar relations: decades of painstaking negotiations between humans and Kalgzar finally brought to a successful conclusion. The physical limits of space-time had dictated a glacial pace of progress as the two different species fumbled to understand each other.

But the much anticipated first contact had exploded into one giant, fetid mess, and someone would catch the blame for it. Ortiz drummed his fingers on the table. As lead security operative for the Kalgzar party, he had a good idea who would be the sacrificial lamb. He was impatient for her to arrive, if only to have someone else to share the burden with.

The door swung open and a small woman strode in, her feet almost soundless against the gleaming parquet flooring. She examined Ortiz and Guzik, settling on Ortiz as the leader.

"You're the fool who called for help over this trivial piece of stupidity?"

Ortiz choked on his coffee; she obviously had no idea of the seriousness of what had happened.

"You *are* Casteneda?"

"How many people did you invite?" Casteneda's black eyes locked with his.

"Shouldn't have even invited you," Guzik grunted, his ever-present sunglasses reflecting Casteneda's gaunt face.

"No need for that, Dan. Ms. Casteneda is well known for solving tricky problems." He turned back to her and shivered; there was something imperious and threatening in her haggard features. "You know what's happened?"

"My dear man, the entire conscious world is aware of what happened. The 3V recording even made it through to *me*, despite the filters I have in place to block anything related to popular culture."

"But, if you know…" Ortiz was even more confused. How could she dismiss it so casually?

"Let me convince you." Casteneda perched on the edge of a chair, looking as though she was almost part of the collection of dusty legal tomes that filled the shelves behind her. Her shock of black hair gave her the appearance of an ancient Raven — ready to pounce at any sign of weakness.

"One — we were receiving the first in-person Kalgzar

delegation. Two — the delegation was received at its starship by a party led by an air-headed idiot with the improbable name of Fawnda, whose only 'qualification' seems to be a generously endowed chest. Three — the Kalgzar ambassador, Dh'Aht, upon meeting this Fawnda, promptly attacked her, tearing off what little clothing she was wearing and sexually assaulting her in public."

The small scar on Ortiz's left cheek visibly whitened as he grimaced at her bluntness. Casteneda simply ticked off the next finger.

"Four — the public with its usual sense of misplaced gung-ho optimism, has called for the immediate destruction of the Kalgzar. Five — the Kalgzar delegation has returned to its ship and has ignored all communication attempts. Six — the security services are so incompetent that they call out a Systems Engineer to help with a diplomatic issue."

"You were highly recommended, someone who could be trusted. We were told-"

"Forget what you were told. In all my years the only thing I have ever done is think. It's something I would strongly encourage you to try, at least once in your life."

"You think we should just let those tentacled freaks get away with this?" Guzik thumped the table with a meaty hand. "They shouldn't have been allowed to come here."

"First contact is often a bloody affair." Casteneda frowned. "Whose brilliant idea was it to put the silicone-enhanced Fawnda in charge of the greeting party?"

"It was a request from the Kalgzar." Ortiz shuffled uncomfortably. "They're fascinated by Earth popular culture; they have nothing like it. Fawnda is the leading 3V superstar; her shows are rated number one around the world."

"I love 'Get it on with Fawnda!'. What a babe!" Guzik's broad grin slowly faltered at Casteneda's expression. "I guess you... never saw that one..."

"So, what do you expect me to do?" Casteneda looked like she'd stepped in something unpleasant. "I don't imagine

'Fawnda' is exactly unused to having her clothing removed. Once she's calmed down, stage an apology by the Kalgzar and I'm sure everyone will soon forget they've been insulted. I'm no diplomat, as I am sure you've realized by now."

"You don't understand." Ortiz rubbed his forehead. "Ever since we made contact with the Kalgzar we've been fighting prejudice. They errr... don't look like us and that's triggered some 'unrest'. We call it the 'evil-alien syndrome'."

"It would be virtually impossible for a separate line of evolution to create something vaguely similar to humans. Who would imagine that they would?"

"Well, on 3V, aliens always appear pretty much like us. It's created an expectation that..."

"You're telling me that people actually base their idea of extra-terrestrial life on 3V shows?"

"Worse. Creatures with tentacles..." Ortiz coughed. "Well, they tend to be the bad guys."

Casteneda sighed. "Whenever I think I've seen the worst of human stupidity, something reminds me that I haven't."

"It may be irrational." Ortiz shrugged. "But we have to deal with it. It's a sensitive issue for the Kalgzar."

"That's hardly surprising." Casteneda folded her hands in her lap. "They mastered interstellar travel while humans were still struggling to cross open water in hide-wrapped boats. They've advanced us technologically and culturally. And what is our return to them? We resent them and think of them as monsters."

"This is what those damn aliens were after all along. They've been setting us up." Guzik fingered the gun at his waist. "We should take 'em out. Teach them they can't walk in here and start raping our women."

"Of course..." Casteneda's lips were a tight line. "We have our own 'men' for that."

Guzik jumped up from his chair. "I don't have to-"

"You're right, you don't." Ortiz's teeth crunched slightly as his jaw tightened. "You're reassigned as of now. Get back to the office and wait for your next duty."

Guzik's mouth opened and closed twice. Then, without another word, he stomped past Casteneda, leaving behind only the overpowering scent of his aftershave. The sound of office workers busy in adjacent rooms seemed thunderous in the silence that followed.

"Sorry. That's the kind of thinking we have to worry about. He's not a bad man, but this situation has everyone wound up. We need to find something that will tell the world they have nothing to fear from the Kalgzar."

"Do you really believe that to be the case?" Casteneda asked. "They have the power to travel from one star-system to another; they could undoubtedly wipe us out easily."

"They're just not like that. You don't know Dh'Aht. He wanted this meeting so much. He genuinely thought humans and Kalgzar could help each other."

"Even if what you say is true, that in itself could be seen as suspicious. They're far more advanced. What could we possibly give them?"

"I'm not sure exactly; it was a cultural thing from what I could tell. Dh'Art once said the Kalgzar were tired; as a race they needed to learn from our dynamism and inquisitiveness." Ortiz hesitated. "Of course, the Agency and the High Council is worried we've offended them so much that we *do* have to fear them."

Casteneda was silent for several moments. "Will they talk to me?"

"I don't know. They haven't responded to any of our signals."

"Remote communication isn't the answer. I need to talk to them face-to-face."

"They don't really have faces as such." Ortiz's smile crumbled slowly against Casteneda's long silence.

"The first thing is to understand what happened. Get me transport to their ship."

The Kalgzar ship dominated the south side of the airport. It was the only available area both big enough and reasonably secure. Casteneda felt like an ant next to a garbage can as she strode towards the main hatch.

To her surprise, the hatch started to swing out as she approached and by the time she reached it several Kalgzar were waiting for her.

One of the group slid forward, the underside of his tentacled body undulating rhythmically. The Kalgzar didn't have legs as such. They resembled purple fleshy fire hydrants, a curtain of tentacles running all the way around their circumference, with no visible eyes and a large sharply-toothed mouth.

"I First Command Lr'Rax. Forgive, I trained not Earth speak. We know not you."

"I'm Casteneda. The Security people asked me to talk to you. They're worried about what you'll do. This is a bad thing."

"Yes. Yes. Bad, bad thing. We know much shame. Much much shame. Come."

Lr'Rax led Casteneda through a series of low arched corridors; Kalgzar were only around a meter tall and Casteneda had to stoop as she moved. There was an odor that she couldn't place, a mix of burnt rubber tinged with the metallic overtone of ozone and she forced herself not to wrinkle her nose.

Eventually they stopped in a widened area bordered on one side by a transparent wall. It wasn't glass or anything solid, but Casteneda sensed that nothing would pass through it.

On the other side of the wall a Kalgzar was strapped to the floor.

"Dh'Art?" Casteneda pointed at the figure.

"Yes. Dh'Art" Lr'Rax guided her closer with a gentle pressure to her hand. "Talk. Dh'Art."

She stopped a few centimeters from the wall. There was a pulsing sound, almost inaudible and Casteneda wasn't sure if it was coming from the equipment around her or if it was something more powerful at a distance. "Dh'Art? Do you hear me? I'm Casteneda. I'm here to help if possible."

"Casteneda? Human? Scum human. How *dare* you talk to me! You and all other Earth creatures. Scum. You will all die! You do not deserve our help. Why should we help such inferior creatures? We should destroy you. Eat you. Ravage you. Let me out. Let me have this human and I will show you how to treat such low born sc'llz. Let me have her. Let me have-"

One of the other Kalgzar touched a wall panel and Dh'Art slumped lower, his gray leathery skin relaxing into a slight pulsating movement. Some kind of sedative, thought Casteneda.

"Cs'neda. Here."

Lr'Rax indicated a blank wall and Casteneda examined it closely. Their visual sense was obviously very different — this was going to be harder than she'd thought.

"I don't see anything."

Lr'Rax manipulated something unseen and an area of the wall phased through different colors and shapes. Then the outline of a Kalgzar appeared.

"That's it. Good."

Lr'Rax changed the controls and Casteneda watched in fascination as the image seemed to peel back layers of the subject on display.

"Dh'Art?"

Lr'Rax shivered, his fringe of tentacles vibrating and Casteneda guessed that the movement was the equivalent of a nod.

The image changed again, revealing a loaf-shaped mass of tissue. On one side of the loaf was a throbbing blue lump that somehow appeared out of place, even though Casteneda didn't know the first thing about Kalgzar anatomy.

"Dh'Art. Thinkplace." Lr'Rax hesitated. "Computer, not mineral. Flesh. Main Kalgzar part."

"That's his brain?"

"Yes. Brain." A tentacle stretched out to the display and brushed the blue pulsing area. "Not brain. Bad. Hurt brain. Change Kalgzar."

Casteneda took a deep breath, a sense of excitement and relief rushing through her. "Of course!"

"From what I understand, it's a form of swelling on the brain. It rarely happens in Kalgzar, but when it does it changes their personalities completely. They become forceful, belligerent and, as everyone saw, subject to frenzied behavior." Casteneda waited patiently for the information to sink in.

"This just happened?" Ortiz hastily activated his DataPad and scribbled a few notes. "Sorry, I'm relaying this directly through to the Agency and the High Council. They need to know."

"It must have been there for some time. Usually the Kalgzar involved is the first to know and arranges for treatment. In this case it seems that Dh'Art was overtaken by his determination to complete the diplomatic mission and ignored the warning signs."

"Will he recover?"

"They're not sure. If it's caught early they can treat it, but in Dh'Art's case it may be too far advanced."

Ortiz shook his head. "Poor guy. We need to get this message out. No one can blame the Kalgzar if their representative is ill. But how do we make it clear?"

Casteneda smiled for the first time. "I might be able to help with that."

Around the world the rumor mill and calls for action faded as the official story was pumped vigorously into every channel; headlines proclaiming the news.

"Abcess Makes Dh'art Grope Fawnda!"

The End

My work contract ended temporarily and gave me the opportunity to focus on writing – a true luxury and one I grabbed eagerly. I enjoy a good feghoot after reading several by the master, Isaac Asimov. Wikipedia describes a feghoot as "a humorous short story or vignette ending in an atrocious pun (typically a play on a well-known phrase) where the story contains sufficient context to recognize the punning humor. A little time spent musing over a suitable pun gave me my ending and I realized that Castenada was the perfect character to offset the silliness of the pun. Castenada first appeared in my story "Reboot" and I loved her bristling, no-prisoners-taken acerbic attitude. I knew somehow that I'd have to revisit her.

He Who Controls

Tom Sheetman buzzed through to his secretary. "I'd like to talk about the report on Finister and Sons, Miss Logie."

"I'll be there in a few minutes."

Tom turned to his computer and checked his clippings on the flat screen. He was late for a deadline and it wasn't the first time. If he didn't get something together by the afternoon Logie would be jumping all over him. She was a first class bi-

"Sheetman? Have you checked the main line flow? It's backed up like a sewer and there's going to be hell to pay." Logie sounded harsher through the desk speaker than she did in real life.

"I'll put a repair crew on it right away."

Tom slashed his hand through the holoscreen to blank the display and strode over to the window. People scurried through the gray concrete streets below, but he found it almost impossible to focus. His head ached; the mindless throng shifted and reformed, like an ever changing monster consuming everything it touched. He rubbed his forehead, his fingers rasping against the smooth skin.

"Mr. Sheetman? This *is* important."

Tom turned to see a slight, rat-faced man sat by his desk. "Yes? Sorry, of course it is, Mr. Colby."

"This is the fifth consecutive period your company has

defaulted. I'm afraid the bank can't allow this to continue."

There was something wrong with the conversation, but Tom couldn't put his finger on it. "You'll get paid, but I'm not going to lay people off." Some of them had been with him since the first; he wouldn't let them down. "We just need time to get through this slump."

"You don't have any more ti-"

Tom doubled up, his stomach on fire as he staggered toward the desk. Colby was gone, but where? Was he hallucinating? Had he eaten something? He slumped into the padded chair and buzzed his admin assistant.

"Please… get my wife on the phone, Miss…" He stopped. What *was* his secretary's name? Then it came to him. "…Miss Benedict, I need her to pick me up"

"I can call her…" Miss Benedict sounded confused. "But your divorce went through last week, remember?"

Divorce? Tom's whole body started to shake uncontrollably. What the hell was happening? "I'm taking the afternoon off. Please cancel my meetings."

"Meetings?" The pleasant male baritone on the speaker paused. "Sorry, you are?" The line clicked several times and then went dead.

Tom ran from his office and threw himself into the nearest elevator. He heard a ripple of shouts behind him, but couldn't pick out individual voices. He fought to press the right button on the elevator as his hands trembled. The elevator rattled several times, then stopped in the basement garage. A faint smell of gasoline and oil caught in Tom's nostrils when the doors opened, almost making him vomit. He hurried over to his car, scrabbling in his pocket for the key. He reached to open the door and stopped. His hand was empty, though he was sure the key had been there a moment earlier.

The red Porsche definitely wasn't his. It was in his spot, but his car was… His head pounded as he tried to remember his car's color. Blue? Silver? The dingy lights made it difficult to make things out clearly, but it didn't matter. Whatever the color, it sure wasn't a Porsche. It was a-

Tom shook his head. His heart felt like it was pumping straight into his temples, the wet pounding sending waves of nausea through his stomach.

How stupid, he thought. He hadn't brought a car, that's why he didn't have the keys. No-one with any sense drove in the city. He'd come on the Metro like any sane person. The station was only a block away on Fifth. An easy walk, even in the worst weather.

"You there!"

Tom turned and saw a security guard approaching, the crispness of his uniform at odds with the stubble on the man's jaw.

"What are you doing?" The guard danced his flashlight beam from Tom to the car and back. "That's not your vehicle, is it?"

"I don't… That is, I'm not sure… I think, maybe…"

The guard stepped closer, his name badge coming into view as he walked under one of the few working bulbs.

"Logie?" The name seemed familiar, but Tom's thoughts seemed to fall apart when he tried to think about such details.

"Do I know you?" The guard squinted at Tom then winced, grunting heavily. "What the…"

The guard doubled up and Tom moved instinctively to help him. But before he could, a dark-blue Nissan squealed to a halt beside them.

"Tom? Are you okay?"

Tom didn't recognize the car or driver, but any escape from the guard's suspicious scowl seemed like a sanctuary. He lurched towards the car and jerked the passenger door open, then hesitated. What if the guy in the car was some kind of weirdo? His eyes closed as he felt the pressure of his own attempt to think dissolve into chaos.

"My friend isn't well," the stranger called out. "He called me to pick him up… must have forgotten."

The guard fingered his radio. "Maybe… he's acting real

suspicious. Like-"

Silence.

Tom looked around. The guard had vanished, almost as if he'd never been there; the Porsche was also gone. Even the garage lighting seemed brighter; the grimy, yellowed bulbs were somehow now overhead strip-lights.

"Get in. If you value your sanity—get in the car."

"Do you recognize me?"

"Should I?" Tom was grateful his stomach had started to settle since sinking into the passenger seat.

"Alan Ballo." He guided the car into the first auto-drive lane, released the controls and turned to face Tom. "You don't remember me?"

Tom examined Ballo's broad features, but had no recollection of seeing him before. "Are you a friend of my wife's?" It was a question driven by social instinct only.

"I'm a friend of *yours*, actually." Ballo seemed disappointed. "I was hoping you'd remember me at least. I guess our paths don't intersect in this 'now'. Whatever that is."

The cars around them flickered. Tom tried to focus on them, but couldn't. His head started to ache again and he wasn't the only one; when they stopped at an intersection he saw a man convulsing at the side of the road. The cars and people seemed to change shape, size, and even number as he watched. The buildings alongside the road were similarly indistinct, as if they couldn't quite decide what shape to be.

The street branched sharply. Tom found himself pinned against the inside of the door as the car skidded around the abrupt turn. Ballo swore and wrestled with the controls, finally switching the Auto-drive back on when the street seemed to stabilize.

"Temporal shock-waves are affecting everything, including basic infrastructure. It was a risk using the car, but I didn't have much choice. I'm not sure how long we have left."

"Left? This is a gag, right? Are we being filmed?" Tom

glanced around trying to spot any hidden cameras. "Did my brother put you up to this?"

Ballo's wide brow furrowed, "If only. I was trying to block quantum noise to study dark energy. I'd just fired up the shield to do preliminary tests at my lab. That's when I saw everything around me doing this." Ballo gestured at the ephemeral view around the car. "The shield didn't work the way I expected. Instead of blocking quantum noise it blocked the temporal shifts."

"Tempura what? Please don't mention food...." Tom held his stomach, which was still a little upset from earlier.

"Temporal. As in *time*." Ballo sounded annoyed. "Time shifts are occurring constantly. I think there's some kind of unusual resonance or feedback happening that's-"

"Time shifts? You mean as in time travel? So you're a scientist working on time-travel? Look, I'm not that stupid. Let me out here — the joke's over. Tell Jimmy I'll punch his lights out if he's lost me my job."

"Please." Ballo put his hand on Tom's knee, but pulled away abruptly when Tom stiffened. "This will be difficult, but I need you to believe me. We're almost at the lab. Give me a chance to explain to you calmly — after that you can just walk away if you want. I won't stop you. Just ten minutes."

Tom thought about how the security guard and Porsche had vanished, the strange scenes in the streets. It must have been a trick, but he was damned if he could figure out how it was done. "Okay, ten minutes."

Ballo nodded, his dark features relaxing a little. "Thanks."

"So how do you claim to know me?"

"As I said… we're friends."

"I don't have any scientist friends. I'm pretty sure I'd know if I did." Tom felt bad when Ballo flinched. "Unless you count my Uncle Frank. He said he'd been abducted by aliens and given special mind powers. Don't suppose that really counts."

"I never met him."

"So how did *we* meet?"

"At a party. Your sister's thirty-fifth birthday. I was a friend of a friend, invited along to make up numbers."

Tom wondered if he'd been drunk at the time; a family party made that a distinct possibility. "So we met at Theresa's?"

"Sarah's." Ballo looked away.

"I don't have a sister called Sarah."

"You did." Ballo turned back to the controls, taking over as the auto-drive system cut out. He drove down an exit ramp with a large sign announcing they were entering the Tren-Hump Institute for Advanced Physics.

"It used to be the Kirschner Institute," Ballo muttered.

They hurried inside. Tom wasn't sure what to expect; there were no giant machines covered with flickering lights or banks of dancing laser beams, just a series of very drab, gray offices. Ballo ushered Tom through a door and locked it behind them.

Tom drew back. "Wait a sec... I'd prefer you left that-"

Ballo thrust the key into Tom's hand, his hands lingering against Tom's briefly before pulling back. "Don't worry. You're safe."

Tom looked around; the office walls were bare except for several framed awards with Ballo's name on them. A large desk containing a very ordinary looking computer sat at one end, but at the far end of the lab was a bench overflowing with a hotchpotch of unusual instruments. He walked towards them. They were the only thing he'd seen so far that piqued his interest and that he might identify as "research tools."

"Don't!" Ballo leapt towards Tom.

"I wasn't going to touch them."

"The equipment?" Ballo took a deep breath. "Oh, that doesn't matter. The shield only extends a few meters. If you'd stepped outside it you'd have been gone."

"What the hell are you talking about?"

"The shield protects us from time shifts." Ballo pulled a small box out of his pocket and held it up; it glowed blue at both ends. "But it was designed to go around instruments, not people."

"You're not making any sense."

Ballo half fell into the worn leather chair beside the desk. He massaged his temples with his fingers, stroking up into his gray speckled hair. "You've heard of ChronSkeetas?"

"No…"

There was a picture frame on Ballo's desk which he hastily pushed inside a drawer. Then he rolled his head from side to side, easing the tension in his shoulders. "Maybe they're called something else for you. Small devices that go back in time to take pictures. They look like insects and weigh about the same."

"You mean Time-Bugs like historians use? Why didn't you say that? They're fun. I've got a few videos of myself when I was a toddler bumping into all kinds of things."

"Yes, I've seen them."

It seemed as if Ballo had been about to say more then stopped himself and Tom frowned. The videos weren't the kind of thing shared with just anyone. "So what about the Time-Bugs?"

"They're destroying civilization."

Tom guffawed. "Okay, okay. I may not be a scientist, but I'm not stupid either." He was about to walk away, but hesitated when he remembered Ballo's earlier comments about the size of the shield. "Those things are harmless."

"That's what the manufacturers claimed: they're small, harmless, and very limited. That doesn't make it true."

Tom felt stupid for listening and checked his watch. "They can't change anything. They record video and stuff and come back."

Ballo stood up and clasped his hands behind his back. "The energy requirements limit time-jumps to approximately seventy-five years. When they run out of power the devices snap back to the time of launch with their images stored."

"Right, so how can that hurt anything?" Tom was getting annoyed. Ballo sounded like some crackpot scientist from a 3V show. He checked his watch again. "Are you done?"

"This isn't my field, you understand. This is a theory I've

constructed over the last few weeks."

"Weeks?"

"That's when I switched this on." Ballo pointed to the blue-glowing box on his desk. "Before that I was as ignorant as everyone else. Let me show you."

Ballo switched on the 3V at the far side of the room. It lit up, but the image was distorted. Everything had a curious ghosting effect that made the people look unreal and the sound was just a garbled mess, so confused that Tom couldn't pick out a single word. Ballo switched channels repeatedly; each one was the same.

"Okay, your 3V is broken. Time I was leaving." He moved towards the door.

"How do you explain what you saw on the way over?"

Tom hesitated. He'd definitely seen some strange things outside and his own experiences were disconcerting by any standards. Even as he tried to remember the earlier part of the morning he felt his thoughts become ragged. "Maybe your cockamamie shield distorts things. How would I know?"

"How about this?" Ballo typed something on his computer and turned the screen around so Tom could see it. Do you recognize that?"

"It's the City website." Tom scanned the screen. "Who's Mayor Starck?"

"I have no idea. It was Keenan the last I knew."

"That's a fake. Carlew won by a landslide. Everyone knows that."

"It's not fake — the timeline has been altered. If we moved the shield generator away from the computer it would change and someone else would be elected. Maybe the person you remember, or mine."

"I never heard so much garbage in my life. I'm leaving." Tom moved towards the door.

"Wait! What do you do? Your occupation?"

The answer should have come easily, but somehow Tom found himself confused. "I'm an… engineer." The word trailed away even as he said it.

"In my reality you were a journalist."

"That's as crazy as everything else you've said. I can't spell and I don't even type very well."

Ballo tapped on the computer again. A page appeared from the Tribune with Tom's picture next to the headline.

"The Realities Of Production For Use - Tom Sheetman."

"That could be faked too. This is nuts. If Time-Bugs were dangerous they'd be banned. And if they were being used to change time like you say, the Government would step in and do something — change it back the way it was."

"How would they know? From what I can see, no one exposed to the changes notices. They'd need a shield like this one and I created it for my research; it's the only one."

Tom felt his palms moisten and his armpits getting sticky. The pale blue walls momentarily imploded. He swallowed hard, fighting off the claustrophobic sensation and sat heavily in a chair across from Ballo. This crazy scientist seemed to have an answer for everything. "But t's a time jump generator and a camera, that's it…"

Ballo steepled his fingers. "It was hard to pin down because of the constant changes, but someone reverse-engineered them and published the plans on the Net."

"ChronSkeetas, or *Time-Bugs*, are usually simple, as you said. All they have is a body to provide limited movement, a tiny camera and enough memory to hold a couple of minutes of reasonable quality 3V."

"Right, that's what I thought." Tom's jaw tightened; he still wasn't convinced.

"But the plans have spawned different variants. And at least one of them has switched things around. The 'Skeeta doesn't record; it *projects*."

"Projects what?"

"Images, 3V, documents. Whatever's in its memory."

Tom rubbed his chin. Ballo was just too quick for him to catch out. "Why would anyone do that?"

"Think about it. How many mistakes have you made in your life that you wish you could undo? How often would a little bit of advance knowledge have changed things for the better? A Skeeta could easily hold enough sporting results that you could become a multi-millionaire by betting on them. Or stock movements, company acquisitions… Or how about simply avoiding a bad relationship before it begins? Or perhaps you don't like who was elected…"

"But?"

"Anything can be changed and *is*. How much does a ChronSkeeta… a Time-Bug cost?"

"I don't know. Sixty, maybe seventy bucks?"

"I remember them closer to a hundred, but the point is that price is no barrier. Who wouldn't scrape or steal that kind of money to turn their life around?"

The door opened and a mirror image of Ballo walked in.

"What the hell?" Tom looked from one man to the other. They were identical.

"Ahhh the star-crossed lovers. I'm glad I caught you both." The second Ballo sauntered closer and jerked his thumb at Tom. "Did you tell him yet?"

"Tell me what? Are you two twins?" Tom stood and backed away; this was getting crazier by the minute.

"Tom, remember the shield," the first Ballo cautioned, then turned to the second. "How did you get here?"

"The same as you, of course." Ballo Two held up a metal box identical to the one on the desk. "Did you think you'd be the only version of you to come up with this?"

Ballo One scooped up the shield from his desk. The dark skin on his fingers whitened as he held it tight. "I suppose that makes sense and explains how you have a duplicate UNICA door-key."

"I'm nothing like you though. You're full of romantic crap. I mean really, you want to save the world *and* your boyfriend? I'm much more practical." Ballo Two wandered across the office, surrounded by an iridescent soap-bubble of light, and looked at the lab equipment. "I have to say, it *is* kind of creepy how much this looks like my lab."

Ballo Two bent low over the equipment. "Interesting. You put a feedback loop in the quantum stream. I thought of that, but didn't think it would work. Anyway, that's not why I'm here."

Ballo One sneered. "Let me see if I can guess. You represent certain nameless parties who are making a lot of money from the current situation and want it to continue." He spat out the words.

Ballo Two laughed. "You're almost as smart as I am, but not smart enough."

"And how are you going to stop me?"

Ballo Two reached into his pocket and pulled out a pistol. "Like I said, I'm very practical."

Tom's hand flashed out and grabbed Ballo Two's wrist, slapping it against the hard edge of the steel desk. The gun skittered to the floor and Ballo One picked it up, using two fingers as if it were something dirty.

Tom locked his arms around Ballo Two and looked across at Ballo One. "Two years of self-defense classes. Never thought I'd need to use it."

Ballo Two snarled, staring at the gun in his duplicate's hand. "Are you going to use that on me? Tenford isn't going to be happy about this and killing me won't stop him."

Ballo One came around the desk and pulled the shield generator out of Ballo Two's pocket, brandishing it in front of his twin. "This is all we need."

"Wait! No, you can't!" Ballo Two wrenched against Tom's grip, nearly breaking the hold. "Shoot me, but don't do that."

"Push him over there, Tom." Ballo One pointed to the doorway with the pistol. "We don't need to hurt him."

Tom twisted Ballo Two around and pushed him away. Ballo Two staggered forward. As he approached the door he seemed to blur, becoming increasingly shadowy until he simply vanished.

"Where'd he go?"

"It's impossible to say. Back into the random froth of time-based probabilities."

"Is what he said true?" Tom frowned. "You and me were..."

Ballo shrugged. "It doesn't matter. Not anymore. That was a completely different timeline."

"But that's why you err... rescued me?"

"I hoped I'd find the Tom I knew, or at least one who recognized me."

Tom felt awkward and almost wished Ballo hadn't saved him. He felt nauseous again, but in a much different way to how he'd felt just before meeting Ballo. How could that be? He'd never felt even the slightest urge that way. Hell he was married, or was he? The confusion from earlier seemed to encircle him again momentarily and he swallowed hard; how could anyone possibly think about such things rationally. "You must have cared a lot about him... me...."

Ballo shuffled the papers on his desk. "We need to get on; we don't have a lot of time."

"That sounds like a contradiction in the circumstances."

Ballo held up the metal box. "The power cells are nearly dead."

"Can't you change them?"

"Then the power would be interrupted and this bubble of reality will vanish along with both of us."

"This might have more power." Tom held up the second generator, then whistled. "But then your timeline would end — you wouldn't exist anymore. Not this version of you anyway."

"Yes, the temporal bubble inside will be different."

Tom thought about it. "The world might be a better one than yours was."

"It's something I've considered." Ballo turned and took a step away. "I've no idea if my time represents the 'real' version or not. It's not important anymore. The world I knew is gone regardless."

"From what you've said it sounds like the pieces may

get jumbled, but things are largely the same overall — same people, same places. Is that so bad?"

"I had an intuition, a hunch." Ballo looked sheepish. "I don't know what exactly. Some research suggests the brain has a quantum component, which may explain consciousness. If time shifts happen at a quantum level, then they could impact the brain."

Tom laughed. "Did we communicate any better when I knew you? I swear I've no idea what you're talking about."

"Sorry. You've said similar things to me before. If the shifts in the time-line are affecting the brain, then I wondered if there'd be any visible signs." Ballo tapped something into the computer.

Tom looked at the search results. They discussed unusual cases of mental problems occurring randomly, often in people with no previous history of such issues. "The shifts…?"

Ballo nodded. "The data isn't certain, but it looks like frequent time-shifts are increasing levels of schizophrenia and other psychotic disorders."

Tom leaned closer to read the descriptions. "This is *your* version of reality though. Couldn't it be different in others?"

"When I leave the computer it 'updates' with the new reality. I see the same type of results each time. The rapid shifts are affecting quantum brain processes, slowly destroying normal functioning. From what I can tell, it's getting worse."

"Is there anything you… we can do?"

"I'm going to change time."

Tom snorted. "Isn't that what started all this?"

"I know it's counter-intuitive, but it's the only solution I can think of; as long as the shifts continue it's hopeless. Willard Kinker invented the ChronSkeeta. I've managed to pinpoint when he first tested it. If I send back the shield to envelop that event, I think the temporal displacement will be contained and will resonate inside the shield—destroying everything inside."

"And Kinker?"

Ballo looked away. "He'd be caught inside the resonance."

"You mean killed?"

"Actually I've no real idea of what would happen. I don't think he'd die as such, but the event itself would implode in a temporal collapse. His existence, along with the ChronSkeetas, would vanish into a sea of improbabilities."

"That's pretty callous." Tom wondered how anyone could talk so casually about ending someone's existence. "The end justifies the means?"

"What else would you have me do?"

Tom rubbed his eyebrows with his thumbs. His head was throbbing and filled with flashes of strange memories — his wedding and honeymoon, his work as a journalist, but somehow none of it seemed to belong to him. How could he and Ballo have ever got together? They were so different.

Tom felt Ballo's hand on his shoulder and for a moment it was comforting. Then he twisted away. "How would you do it? Send the shield back?"

"According to my calculations it will take at least thirty 'Skeetas. If they're attached to the shield generator, temporal inertia should drag it along with them."

"Should?"

"Yes, *should*. As I said, this isn't my field. It's an educated guess." Ballo snapped the words through tightened lips.

"Don't get angry with me. You brought me into this."

"Sorry. It's been stressful..." Ballo massaged the bridge of his nose. "Especially not being able to talk to anyone."

Tom felt a stirring of sympathy on hearing Ballo's voice crack. It spoke of hours struggling with the problem and how to solve it. He wondered how anyone would stay sane. Imagine knowing the world around you was changing minute by minute and your own existence was no longer real. "Do you have enough Time-Bugs? Sorry, ChronSkeetas..."

"I've got two." Ballo's skin darkened at the admission. "I can get more from the stores. They're not hard to pick up."

Tom scowled. "I guess that'll work if we have time. How long will the shield last?"

Ballo sighed. His breathing seemed easier just knowing that Tom accepted what he was saying. "I don't know for sure. I never did any power drain tests. I think we should have a few hours."

"Let's hope that's enough."

Ballo moved around the desk and stopped, his shoulders falling. "You don't have to do this."

"What else is there?"

"You could step outside the shield."

Tom hesitated. "Where would I end up? I wouldn't go back to where I was, would I?"

"You'd go back into the quantum froth of space-time, like the other version of me."

Tom wondered how it would be: a new life, a new Tom, new everything. "What the hell… the Twisters are on a losing streak anyway. Call me selfish, but I kind of like the person I am."

Ballo nodded and they moved towards the door in unison. As he opened it a soldier strode towards them, surrounded by a shimmering soap-bubble. Ballo pulled Tom back behind the door, locking it again.

Tom's face was pale. "He had a gun."

"It looked like it. We need to-"

The door burst open. The soldier sprang through and raised a boxy rifle, aiming it directly at Ballo. His finger was already squeezing the trigger.

Tom stepped in front of Ballo as the gun went off and a bright flash surrounded him. He leapt backward with a yelp. The smoldering remains of the shield generator he'd been holding crashed to the floor where it hissed and sparked.

The soldier hesitated at the pyrotechnic display, then raised his rifle again.

Three explosive blasts sounded behind Tom and his whole body clenched. The soldier crumpled, bloody stains soaking through his uniform. Tom whirled around to see Ballo holding the pistol, a torpid curl of smoke drifting from the barrel.

"What the hell?"

"I didn't even think. He was going to fire again. The gun was on the desk and I…" Ballo slumped down into the chair, the seat squeaking under him.

"What happened?" Tom edged up to the body on the floor and picked up the odd looking rifle. "What kind of gun is this?"

Ballo reached into his desk and pulled out a small bottle partly filled with a clear liquid. He took a gulp, then offered it to Tom. "I think it's designed to pierce the shield and make it collapse. You were holding the other shield. When he fired, *that* field collapsed, but luckily we were still isolated in mine."

Tom took the bottle, but the smell of alcohol mixed with the acidic gun-smoke made him nauseous. They'd just killed a man. He handed the bottle back untouched. "Someone is hunting us now?"

Ballo wiped his forehead. "Presumably the same person that sent the other Ballo — Tenford — whoever that is."

"But why?"

Ballo stumbled over to the body. Rifling through the soldier's pockets he found another shield generator and deactivated it. The soldier and gun vanished. "He who controls the past controls the future. He who controls the present controls the past."

"What's that?"

"Never mind. There'll be more coming after us. I don't see how we can avoid them and get the ChronSkeetas we need."

Tom shivered. "That seems unlikely."

"That's it then. We're beaten." Ballo slouched down in the chair. "We can wait for them to come and get us, wait for the shield to run out. Or just switch it off and who knows what will happen."

"There must be something…" Tom looked helpless. "You're a scientist, dammit."

Ballo gave a soft laugh. "Sometimes I see every bit of him in you. The only thing I regret is not getting a message through to you… *him* before all this. If only to say goodbye. It was our one year anniversary."

Ballo pulled the picture frame out of his desk and handed it to Tom. It showed the two of them in a restaurant, smiling with arms around each other's waist.

"Why did you wait so long? You said it had been weeks."

"I couldn't find any of your other analogs. I sat outside your work for days waiting to catch a glimpse of you."

"That makes me uncomfortable. I wish you wouldn't-" Tom stopped, then thumped the desk. "Wait! *We* control the present."

Ballo looked confused. "Sorry, I don't-"

"The Time-Bugs. You said they can be modified to deliver a message instead of a recording?"

"Yes. That's the problem."

"Couldn't we modify one and send it back to this Kinker guy? Tell him about the disaster they've caused? Are causing? Will cause?" Tom scratched his ear. "It's hard talking about this stuff. If he's a responsible person, wouldn't he hide the discovery? Everything would revert to the original time-line, wouldn't it?"

"That's a big assumption. What if he doesn't care?"

"We'll *make* him care. Explain everything about the mental problems the shifts are causing. How people live almost like ghosts, that nothing is solid anymore."

Ballo scowled. "What if it doesn't work?"

"We'll tell him we have the shield too. That we can send it back to destroy him and the prototype. And if he doesn't knuckle under, that *will* be the next thing we send."

"We can't do that though without the ChronSkeetas."

Tom smiled. "Sure, but he won't know that."

Ballo modified the ChronSkeeta while Tom worked on the message. It was simple enough, a basic text document that would project onto the nearest surface for Kinker to see. Both worked in a determined silence, the pistol ready on the desk, but no-one bothered them.

"It's done." Tom lifted his hands from the keyboard. He smiled and let out a small laugh.

"What is it?"

"I don't know. It's kind of silly, but it feels like we're working on a school science project."

Ballo smiled too. "This will be ready in a few minutes." He made the last-minute microscopic changes needed and uploaded the message. "That's it. The destination is programmed. We're ready."

"Okay, let's go." Tom hesitated. "How will we know if it works?"

"I'm not sure."

"Never mind. Just do it."

Ballo reached out and pressed a key. Nothing seemed to change.

"Did it work?" Tom leaned forward.

Ballo tapped the computer screen "The ChronSkeeta deployed. That's all I can tell you."

A frustrating hour passed, but nothing seemed any different than before. Ballo dug out some stale cookies and they washed them down with bottles of foul-tasting distilled water. It was Tom who finally broke the silence.

"There must be a way to check if anything's happened."

"We could try the 3V. If the shifts have stopped it should be stable."

"Sure. Let's try." Tom swallowed hard. "But I'm not sure I really want to know."

Ballo switched on the 3V and a flickering screen appeared; random half images filled the display accompanied by indecipherable sounds. Tom gasped in defeat behind him.

"Hang on…" Tapping the controls, Ballo switched to another channel.

"…also by lawmakers and political leaders, who said the current system had evolved over decades of political wrangling and could not be revamped easily despite its failure." The news anchorman looked over-tanned and rather bored.

170

"A ten-member investigation team has been created that will look at every aspect of what's needed-"

Ballo switched channel again.

A wide-faced announcer appeared on a sports channel. "Blake Paskerti Rondo returned to action this week following knee surgery twelve weeks ago, but the Chasers insist he is not going to start the game on Friday against the Twisters…"

Tom let out a whoop of victory and hugged Ballo, slapping him several times on the back. "It worked! Damn, it worked!"

"Let's try something else."

They moved towards the computer until it slipped inside the shield's range. Ballo opened a national news page, jotting down the headlines. Then they backed away and returned. The headlines were the same.

"I guess we did it." Ballo sounded surprised. "We *actually* did it!"

"We make a good team." Tom grinned and stepped back. "I'm glad it worked."

Ballo held up the generator. "We can switch this off now. We don't need it anymore."

Tom was quiet for several minutes. "Will we remember any of this?"

"I think we'll be assimilated into the current timeline, but I don't know for sure."

"Will we end up in the same one?"

"I think so."

Tom reached out, grasping Ballo's hand firmly. "I hope we still know each other, wherever we end up."

Ballo lifted his hand and stroked Tom's cheek briefly, then stabbed his finger against the generator's power button.

The End

He Who Controls had a relatively long gestation period (long for me anyway). I started wondering what it would be like if time travel was cheap, uncontrolled and widely accessible, but didn't quite know what to do with the idea for several months. Looking at today's society it seemed obvious that people would use such an ability for entirely selfish reasons. So I started wondering how everyone would want to change things for their own benefit and what it would be like to suffer almost endless shifts in your personal reality. The potential effect that might have on the brain and people's life histories and personalities would be massive and devastating. Later I wondered how it might effect people at a personal level and after sketching out the main character profiles the story almost wrote itself.

One For The Money

"Good morning." Garcia examined the patient's charts and made a small satisfied grunt, moving closer to the alter-like treatment bed that dominated the dimly lit room. "You are Elvis."

"Uh huh."

"Specifically, you're Elvis VII, the seventh produced since this project started. Though the first two were stillborn and technically don't count."

"I'm all shook up." Elvis looked around, his eyes unfocused as if not really taking anything in.

Garcia sighed. "A little disorientation is to be expected. Until ninety minutes ago you were in an Accelerated Growth Chamber. You have been matured to the equivalent of twenty-seven years old. Throughout this process your brain was deliberately isolated while we implanted all memories and personal history available."

"You are not *the* Elvis. You are our product and belong one hundred percent to Real Superstars Incorporated in perpetuity."

"You're the Devil in disguise."

This is going to be more difficult than imagined, thought Garcia. The memory implants need more time to settle. "Get some rest. I'll be back later."

"Thank you. Thank you very much."

Garcia shook his head.

The car pulled up next to the shadowed figure buried in a black trench coat, its headlights casting bright glimmers on the damp asphalt. Garcia wound down the window, grimacing at the smell of stale food and who knew what else that immediately invaded the air-conditioned interior. It wasn't the best of neighborhoods. "Get in."

Elvis crouched, ready to run. "Got a lot o' livin' to do and it ain't happening back at that monkey house. No, sir."

Garcia stepped out and approached with his hand outstretched. His shoes stuck to the pavement with each step and he had to fight to conceal his disgust at what he was stepping in. Elvis had improved, but still had that annoying speech habit. Perhaps it was inevitable given the training, but he wished it would stop. "You've already been spotted. How far do you think you'll get on your own? Several reports have been picked up by the news."

"I'll be home for Christmas." Elvis wiggled his hips. "It's now or never. When I think about what you boys are planning... If I don't get out now, I'll be nothing but your whipped pup forever. I played that role too many times for the Colonel - I ain't doing that again."

A dog howled in the distance and sent chills up and down Garcia's back. He didn't try to point out that the Colonel wasn't part of this Elvis's life. Conversations of that nature only ended in more confusion. "We aren't ready for that kind of exposure yet. These things take proper build up and preparation. Breaking cover now could ruin our plans. You wouldn't want that would you?"

"Don't Cry Daddy. You can make another me in ten minutes, I'm sure."

More like ten years, Garcia thought. Too much acceleration had ruined the previous Elvis versions. If this one didn't work out it would probably be his last chance to complete the project. "Please Elvis. We start performance and recording training next week. You'll enjoy that, it'll be fun."

"That's what you say, but I'm lonesome tonight." Elvis looked away, his eyes low. "You folks plain forgot that there's a whole sentimental me. I'm a man, I don't have a wooden heart."

This again. He'd told the Board they should let Elvis have some companionship, but they thought it would be too much of a distraction. Now it was going to ruin everything. If only he could arrange something. Wait, there was the "sister" project. That would be perfect and she was mature enough now. "Come with me and I'll arrange a treat. A special lady by the name of Paris. She's not much of a conversationalist, but I'm sure you'll find errr... other things to occupy your time."

"Are you sincere?"

"Certainly, my boy. You deserve it."

Garcia smiled. It was a tremendous opportunity and would help Paris IV's development too. How could the Board possibly find a problem with that? It would be controlled and discrete.

"Alright, okay, you win." Elvis barely resisted as Garcia guided him into the warmth of the car.

Garcia burst from the studio, brushing sweat from his forehead. How was it possible? After all the work they'd put in. He had instructions to call the board as soon as the first session ended, but how could he break the news? He leaned against the wall, trying to control his breathing with little success.

His fingers trembled as he punched in the number, hoping no-one would answer. Then the display lit up, showing the Chairman and entire board, their virtual faces floating around the darkened office like ghosts.

"Good day, Mr. Garcia. We've been waiting eagerly." The Chairman laughed. "You're early, so I assume things went well?"

Garcia swallowed hard and tried not to retch.

"I'm sorry, Mr. Chairman. Please give me a minute."

"What's wrong?" The Chairman scowled. "Is there a problem, Doctor Garcia? I thought you'd allowed for all possibilities. You have the best voice coaches, don't you?"

All the voice coaches in the world couldn't fix the caterwauling and incoherent grunts I've just witnessed, thought Garcia. The studio door opened and one of the sound technicians ran towards the restroom, hand clamped across his mouth. For a moment Garcia heard the tortured wails again and tried desperately to shut his ears.

"Good god!" The Chairman's face filled the phone screen. "Was that...?"

Garcia nodded. "Live performances are out of the question, Mr. Chairman. Miming may be possible, but it will require a lot of coaching."

The Chairman waved his fist. "No new material? That will cut potential profits by as much as forty percent. How could you let this happen? You're supposed to be the best. You're finished, do you hear? Finished!"

Garcia withered. Perhaps he should reconsider the Regan proposal, though he hated the idea of working in politics. "There's always an element of risk in genetic manipulation, Mr. Chairman... Perhaps we can use enhancement techniques. The computer guys are getting pretty good at that."

"What good is an Elvis that can't sing, you idiot?" The Chairman reddened. "Is *anything* salvageable? How were his general performance skills?"

Garcia thought hard, searching for the best way to describe the awkward jerky spasms he'd seen. "Well, Mr. Chairman... There *was* a whole lotta shakin' goin' on."

The End

In "*Murphy's Law*", one of the characters was involved in a military operation where she saved "*Elvis VII*". This was meant as nothing more than a random piece of "historical" background to add a little depth to the character — the implication was that somehow Elvis was reborn or cloned. My wife, Hilary, picked up on this and asked right away what the story was behind Elvis VII and when was I going to write it.

I resisted the idea for a long time as I'm really an Elvis fan, but she continued teasing me and bugging me about it. Then — in a flash of inspiration (or madness…) — I had the idea of the clone being programmed with everything from the original Elvis's life and speaking only in song titles. I thought initially that would be hard, but after doing some research, I realized that Elvis had recorded so many songs that it was very achievable. The story almost tumbled out after that.

Uh huh.

Acknowledgments

Thank you for reading. I hope you enjoyed these stories. This book would not have been possible without the help and support of my family, numerous friends (even though many of them think I'm crazy!) and other members of the writing community. I'd like to thank them all (and share the blame). I'd especially like to thank my wife, Hilary, for her constant love, support and patience.

For a complete list of my fiction, please visit my website and consider signing up for my free update newsletter. I will not share your information with anyone for any reason, and won't bombard your mailbox either. I only send updates when I have a new book or special deal for my readers to know about.

The best way to help any writer, especially an indie like myself, is by word-of-mouth. Please consider leaving a review on Amazon. Even if it's only a line or two, it's very much appreciated. Also please look out for other independent authors. There are lots of them out there who work hard to bring you stories that you would never see through commercial publishers.

Thanks again.

David M. Kelly

About the author

David M. Kelly writes intelligent, action-packed SF. He is the author of the novel, Mathematics of Eternity and the short story collection Dead Reckoning And Other Stories. He has been published in Neo-opsis.

Originally from the wild and woolly region of Yorkshire, England, David now lives in wild and rocky Northern Ontario, Canada, with his patient and long-suffering wife, Hilary. He is passionate about science, especially astronomy and physics, and is a rabid science news follower. When not writing, you can find him piloting his own personal starship, a classic 1991 Corvette ZR-1, or exploring the local hiking trails.

Find out more at www.davidmkelly.net

To sign up for the mailing list, go to:
www.davidmkelly.net/contact

You can also follow David through the following channels:

Facebook:facebook.com/David.Kelly.SF
Goodreads: goodreads.com/DavidMKelly
Twitter: twitter.com/David_Kelly_SF

Also Available!

Meet former space engineer, Joe Ballen. These days, he's scraping a living flying cabs in flooded-out Baltimore, trying to avoid the clutches of his boss and the well-meaning advice of an old friend. When one of his passengers suffers a grisly death, Joe is dragged into a dangerous web of ruthless academic rivalry centered on a prototype space-ship. As the bodies pile up, Joe becomes suspect number one, and his enemies will stop at nothing to hide the truth. With the help of an enigmatic scientist, a senile survivalist, and the glamorous Ms Buntin, can Joe untangle the conspiracy and prove his innocence before it's too late?

Mathematics Of Eternity: the first in an explosive SF thriller series by a fantastic new Canadian author.

The future's about to get a lot more action-packed!